Holidays In the Sun.

By

Alex Duggan.

Copyright © Alex Duggan 2025.

Where does the light come from? The same place as the music.

Lord of the Rings cinematographer Andrew Lesnie.

One

Waves warmed by the sun, gently rolled over smooth sand before they folded back into the sea. I had taken to wearing a hat. A straw trilby type. The designer label meant that it cost four times as much as one my wife would have bought me. I wanted an air of classical bohemian elegance. The wife said it was because my hair was thinning, and I would rather look like the mid-life crisis bloke at a BBQ than admit I was getting old.

    She was next to me on a lounger, reading her Kindle. Probably another fantasy romance novel. A semi-human twilight love affair of two lonely souls struggling between two different worlds. I called those books "Werewolf Porn." I preferred to watch David Attenborough, or real porn (ideally not David Attenborough having sex with a wolf). I sat under the shadow of a large straw umbrella, pretending to read a thriller, wearing trilby and sunglasses, secretly watching young women in bikinis walk past. Triple shady. The wife was probably right about the hat.

    As I sat sipping my cocktail, I remembered the old thespian who once told me that no matter what country he was in, it was five o'clock somewhere in the world. Under the gaze of a tropical sun, I held my drink, tapped my ever-expanding belly, and watched the ripples change their size as the girls walked on by. The condensation dripped down the outside of the glass and onto my fingertips. Fuck it. On days like this, life was too short to worry about the calories in my cocktail or the fact that my wife must have shrunk my shirt. I wouldn't mind, but I had bought her that washing machine as a birthday present. I raised my drink and silently toasted the man who had taught me so much about being alive. You see, ever since I was a kid, I always wanted to be an actor.

#

'Who are you?'

'My name,' I said to the police officer. 'Bates. Jack Bates.' It was 1996. I was twenty years old. As I stood there staring into the back of a police traffic van with a speed camera sticking out of it, I should have paid more attention to the police officer. But I was too busy focusing on my performance, the flaw of every young actor when put in front of a lens. Why I had chosen the name of a character I was about to play in a film rather than my real name, I can only say it seemed like a good idea at the time.

'I've always wanted to be in the police.'

The police officer, chief inspector Jerry Bastad, was doing some proactive patrolling to show everyone he was a man of the people. He was certainly a man who hated people. And now he was staring at me, wondering if I could be another juggling monkey in his circus of justice.

'The secret of being a good copper,' he said, 'Is being able to spot when someone is lying. And that means being able to read faces.'

The last word was pronounced in such a way that I immediately thought the man stared at turds. He went on about the importance of having a coppers intuition and being able to know when someone is breaking the law. I thanked him for the advice and left.

Within a few minutes me and my mate Billy Custard were driving around in his crappy car with a pull-out CD player. We went past the mini supermarket, and towards the same speed camera van. We were wearing Ray-bans, black tracksuits, and me sporting a bucket hat. Custard took his Ford Escort up to over forty, beeped his horn, and I stuck my fingers up. We knew the camera would be taking pictures of the car's registration plate, and the speed it was going. A quick trip around the block and we were back, doing exactly the same thing. In fact, we did it a total of eight times. Chief Inspector Bastad sat there next to the camera to make sure he got every single frame.

For me and my mate, it was a celebration of our last day together before I went off for a couple of months. He took me home to say goodbye to my mum, and then I was on my way. A copy of the novel *The Island of Dr Farquar's Fiends,* by T.B. *Wells,* was in my bag, as well as the film script of the same name. Custard dropped me off at the airport. I gave him my ticket for Oasis, who were going to play at Knebworth in a few weeks, and we wished each other good luck.

'Don't come back until you're famous,' he said to me.

'I've only got a little part,' I replied (he had been laughing at that joke since we were twelve).

But the truth was I wanted to get famous. To me, fame was like winning the lottery. It was a chance to buy my parents a big house in the country and take all my friends on expensive holidays. I picked up my bags, my ticket, and started the journey.

Two

> Glory is fleeting, but obscurity is forever.
> Ricky Gervais.

I had an acting age range of sixteen to twenty-six, and had already done some TV shows, but this was the big one. A proper film made on an island location. Inside the airport I got a latte (how much?) and tried to look cool by looking through the film script. I knew my character by heart. I was playing Jack Bates the cabin boy. I had even watched the old film version of the book. A group of people in the 1930s get stranded on an Island run by Dr Farquar, who has spent years experimenting with humans and animals to find the perfect slave. Trying to struggle with my bag, script, and cardboard cup, I spilled some coffee on the front page and my fingers.

'You fucking hot bastard.'

'I am rather lithe for my age,' said an old thespian as he shook my hand. 'It's in my genes, along with my enormous penis. Reginald Kincaid. Who's your agent?'

'Barry Hollocks. I'm playing the part of the cabin boy, Jack Bates. I was recently in -'

The late, great, Reginald Kincaid, a man who had worked in theatre and film since the sixties, smiled serenely (I was to later realise he was probably drunk), and stopped me there.

'Sorry, my fault. I must have been acting like somebody who cares. I know Fufkin. An Israelite whose wife always had a vaginal yeast infection. God knows how, she could barely get a rise out of a Yorkshire pudding. I'm playing Captain Rimlick; the wrinkled old one-eyed salty seaman.' He proceeded to pour some duty-free brandy into both of our coffee's. 'Don't worry. I was a bag of nerves the first time I worked at the film studios in the wood.'

'Hollywood?' I asked.

'No,' Kincaid replied. 'Borehamwood, in Hertfordshire. I stood in front of the camera and gave a wonderful speech, "I have of late—but wherefore I know not—lost all my mirth. That this goodly frame, the earth, seems to me a sterile promontory." Then my mind went blank, and all I could say was "What a piece of shit this is." The director went mad.'

'Because it was Shakespeare?' I said, trying to sound educated.

'No, because I was filming "On the Buses."' Kincaid shook his head. 'But it taught me to be honest with myself first and never drink before the first scene.' He led me towards the seating area. 'How was RADA?'

I didn't tell him I had got into acting the modern way, by becoming an extra, doing a bit of drama at college and then getting a spot in an advert before getting an agent. Going on stage just didn't appeal to me unless it was to win an award. I followed the man who had given over forty years of his life to this venerable institution. Kincaid had a quiet way about him, a walk as if touting for business outside a public lavatory. He had survived the lean years of the seventies, then in the eighties he got a big hit with one film when he went to Hollywood to play what we call "The English bad guy." The sort of person the American hero could kill without a guilty conscience. He had appeared in enough films and TV shows to be one of those actors that you knew you had seen, even if you couldn't remember what it was in. He strolled over to the seating area.

'Let us meet the rest of our players.'

Part of the airport had been taken over by the cast and crew. The riggers, stagehands, and technicians all seemed to be wearing Euro 96 England football shirts and drinking pints. It was ten o'clock in the morning. I sat down and took a sip of coffee, and from the amount of brandy Kincaid had mixed, I wondered if I should join them. Not because of the alcohol in my caffeine, but because I came from those same white working-class streets that most of them had lived in, and my accent was closer to Romford than RADA. My parents were the first in their family's history to buy their own home, and my dad couldn't believe I didn't want to learn a trade. But nobody ever won an award for shovelling shit.

Sitting nearby was Dame Helen Schaffer. She was one of the few female actors who seemed to get more job offers the older she got. At the time I thought it was because she was never that great looking to begin with. She was the Maggie Thatcher of acting, who would play ancient queens and modern bosses all in the same clipped voice. Later I found out I was wrong. Some people just have talent. She got the parts because she was good, and you believed she was the person she was playing. She put down her book of *Bridget Jones Diary* and looked at me.

'Have you done any table work before?'

'I've done quite a few readings,' I lied. 'I'm Liam. I'm playing Jack the cabin boy. I can read through any scenes – ' She stopped me and shook her head. 'I'm terribly sorry Leroy, that's not what meant. Would you be a sweet dear and fetch me a cup of Darjeeling, with just a hint of skimmed milk, not that ghastly UHT stuff. And bring back some serviettes to give the table a clean. Looking at all these big brown ring stains makes me feel like I'm in Rock Hudson's apartment. And a tuna baguette if you get the time. No sweetcorn. They're a devil to wipe away in those tiny airplane toilets. Try the shops over there.' She pointed towards a W.H. Smiths.

And that is when I saw Lara Benson. She had appeared in a few magazines as a ladettes: those women who sit around in lacy underwear talking about football and music. Kids today will never know those pre-internet years of finding a little shop, preferably with an Indian male behind the counter, who would sell you the sort of magazines you held with one hand. Lara was two shelves' down. You never saw the nipples, but you knew they were there. And now I was going to spend a couple of months in the jungle with nothing else to do but sit around watching her in a bikini talking about ball control. I knew she was also going to be in the film. As I got up, Reginald Kincaid handed me a rolled-up magazine.

'Could you return this for me old chap. I've spent so bloody long in this place I've gone through this from cover to cover. If they won't swap it for The Science Weekly or The Spectator, tell them I shall accept a refund.'

I took it and walked over to the shop.

'That was Dame Helen Mivvy,' I said to Lara. 'We're both filming The Island of Dr Farquar's Fiends. I'm Liam Wells. I'm playing Jack Bates. The ships apprentice who helps the others escape from the Island. What about you?

'Panther woman,' Lara replied. 'I only took the part because of Brando Farlow and Sal Klimer.'

I agreed. Farlow was a Hollywood legend, and Klimer was a Hollywood movie star.

Lara shook her head. 'I don't really understand the fascination of fantasy films.' She held up a book. 'This Bridget Jones Diary might be more my part.'

'I agree,' I said, having no idea what she was talking about. 'I'm more into –'I turned to the middle aged white woman behind the counter and unfurled the magazine that Kincaid had wanted me to return, expecting it to be *Sight and Sound*. It wasn't. It was *Busty Grannies, Big Girls Going Bad after the Menopause Edition*. An elderly blonde with breasts like Christmas turkeys adorned the front cover. 'It's not mine. It's.' I turned, but Kincaid had gone.

'For Dame Helen Mivvy?' Lara took it and flicked through the magazine. 'Oh dear. Some of the pages are a bit sticky.' She handed the mag back to me. 'I don't think this is going to be one of those films.'

As she walked away, I knew my first impressions on my fellow actors had not been a good one. But they say a bad rehearsal often leads to a brilliant opening night. As the woman behind the counter asked me if I was old enough to buy *Busty Grannies*, I realised I had fallen in love.

Three

The plane journey consisted of me getting drunk with Reginald Kincaid, and him telling me about the famous people he had slept with. In the sixties and seventies, you had to have sex with everyone to get the part, but it was all kept secret. Now the opposite was true. You slept with someone to get famous and end up on a reality show. Kincaid shook his head.

'How quickly you can go from having someone jizz all over your face, to smiling as some old fart compliments the icing on a cake you've made. The women are just as bad. Stick to films, dear boy, unless you fancy playing some ghastly pleb in a soap. Four years of Shakespeare just to be the pretend you're the manager of a mini market in Cleethorpes when the real job actually pays more.'

Kincaid was as thin as a rake. His capacity to drink could only be described as heroic. He sucked on a cigarette as he pulled out the in-flight magazine.

'Look at this. The bastards are going to ban smoking on all flights from January ninety-seven. Pack us in like sardines, not a problem, but woe betide some trolley haddock who's overdone the lip liner catching you having a crafty suck.

Flying will be worse than prison. At least in there you get to enjoy taking a shit. People will be begging to open the exit door rather than watch another bored air hostess go through the motions of giving the invisible man a hand job.' An air hostess walked past. 'Scrubbers,' Kincaid said under his breath.

She stared at me. It was going to be a long flight.

Kincaid drank and smoked like a convict. I made the mistake of trying to keep up with him. He spoke with a posh accent, and had clearly been to places frequented by the rich and famous. But I think he had only got in by blagging it. I suppose that's why I liked him. Whenever you meet someone and tell them you are an actor, or anything to do with the arts, the first thing you are asked is what you have done; but you know the real question is "How much do you earn?" Reginald was like the Queen. He couldn't give a rat's arse about money. The production company were picking up his bill. He seemed to find me entertaining as well, or rather, I was happy to listen.

Two bottles of red wine later, I was soon asleep. I was woken by Kincaid who had almost polished off another bottle of red wine. He poured some into my plastic cup.

'Don't drink the tea or coffee. The pilots always rub the end of their nob with a finger and then wipe it around the cup of the worse person on the plane. I had a small part in Death in the Clouds. I went up for the role of Poirot. David Suchet got it. He's spent months perfecting the moustache. He told me he based it on the minge of a midget from Eastbourne. You just don't get that sort of dedication from actors anymore.'

The plane juddered, sending half a glass of wine into my lap. I grabbed a magazine and got up to use the toilet. Even though I tries to hide the stain, some of the film crew thought I had pissed my pants and cheered. I stopped next to Lara. She looked at me.

'Are you going to blame that on Reginald Kincaid as well?' I had no reply. I went into the toilet and stared at myself in the mirror. Here I was, a trained actor reduced to the status of a bum, and we hadn't even started filming yet. I took off my jeans and tried to wash the wine out, but it just seemed to spread the stain further, making it look as if I had shit myself as well. I spent ten minutes trying to dry my jeans with some tissues. I put them back on, filling my pants with tissues to help them dry. I came out to the sound of more cheers. As I reached Lara's seat an air hostess tapped me on the shoulder.

'Was everything OK in there?'

'Yes,' I replied. 'But you are probably going to need more tissues.'

At this point I dropped my copy of Busty Grannies. The air hostess stared at the magazine, then the large bulge in my jeans and walked away. And all this time Lara had been watching this little scene. For the rest of the flight, I stayed in my seat.

#

We then had a further journey in a small aircraft and then put on a boat. You could feel the heat even in the shade. In the distance was where we would be calling home for the next few weeks. A tropical island with a single hill. Halfway up the hill was a large white house that was going to be the main set. We docked on a long wooden pier. Stepping on to the Island was like entering paradise. With the soft warm sand, the palm trees, and the sun in the blue sky. I was going to get paid for doing what I love, get a holiday at the same time, and possibly be famous by the end of it.

We were taken to our sleeping quarters. I and a few happy others were to be a band apart. The rest of the cast and crew had their tents situated further into the hot jungle. We actors had our own camp that we would call home. Unfortunately, my agent, Barry Hollocks, hadn't quite told me what was in the small print. Because the production was being filmed in black and white, all our accommodation arrangements had been designed to fit in with a 1930's film. They were large enough to fit a camp bed, wardrobe, desk, and seating area. I thought they were good, but Dame Helen Mivvy was not impressed.

'I didn't win an Oscar playing Hitler's mother just for my arse to become a bouncy castle for mosquitoes.'

Lara checked her mobile phone.

'There's no reception.'

Helen looked around.

'That's because there's no fucking hotel.' She pointed at her tent. 'Look at those. Bigger flaps than Madonna's surgical gown. I must call my agent.'

I noticed that her tent was the largest, the size of a bungalow. Mine was a crestfallen canvas Portaloo. I felt a bony hand on my shoulder.

'In the face of adversity,' said Kincaid, 'One must be like James Bond. Sean Connery. He was a real man. I did a day's work with him once; we must have downed two bottles of gin and a bottle of vodka.'

'What film was you in?' I asked.

'Err, none. I was his caddy at Stoke Golf Club. But he did teach me how to travel like a gentleman.'

Kincaid took me over to his tent. A bar made from wooden crates and four stools were ready to be used. Somehow, a freezer and fridge also sat along the side of his tent. How he got them, and where the electricity came from, I never actually knew. Kincaid had an agent who knew exactly how to treat his star. He put ice into a cocktail shaker and poured in the gin and vermouth.

'Connery said the trick of playing Bond was to realise that it could all be over tomorrow, so always live for the day.' Kincaid got the drinks ready. 'He told me that you have to find the essence of the particular character you are playing; a certain spirit.'
I agreed as.

'I think if I got the chance to play Bond in the future, I would do it with a certain rawness of a man who knew he was going to die but kept to a moral code. Do you know what I mean?'
I nodded, not having a clue what he was talking about. Kincaid pulled out two cocktail glasses from behind the bar. 'Our first martini. To Ian Fleming.'
He knocked his back in one. I followed. The cold gin and dry vermouth slipped down my throat the same way it did for Hemmingway in Paris and Fleming in Barbados.

'Fuck a duck.'

'I've seen that show in Thailand,' said Kincaid. 'And Norfolk. Although I think it might have been a turkey.' He began to make another round of drinks. I looked out across the palm trees. The tropical sea blew in on a gentle breeze. Creatures that did not exist back home buzzed and chirped in the heat of life.

'Connery was the best Bond,' said Kincaid. 'But The Spy Who Loved Me is probably the best film.' He placed a third glass on the bar. 'I almost got the part of Scaramanga. But Christopher Lee had the height. I was then up for Dr Who, but Tom Baker got it. Drank like a fish. The man had the voice of a tenor, and a penis like a trombone; you can't argue with talent like that.'

Helen Mivvy joined us.

'I hope he's not telling you his bloody Scaramouche story?' Kincaid handed her a glass.

'Scaramanga.'

Helen shrugged. 'What's the difference?'

'Well, one is a hitman who uses his golden weapon to kill people; the other is sung by Freddie Mercury on the hit Bohemian Rhapsody.'

Helen took a sip. 'At the Live Aid after show party Freddie was chatting up all the young boys. I showed him my fandango and said I bet even his teeth would have trouble chewing it. Now, tell me Reggie; what on earth is this bloody film all about?'

And so, Reginald Kincaid explained why we were here.

Four

1936. Somewhere in the south Seas. From out of the mist comes an old French steamer, *la Fanny Pourrie*. On board is the one-eyed captain Rimlick (Kincaid), his young cabin boy Jack Bates (me), and a small band of men. The ship has been hired by Lady Ruffsnatch (Dame Helen) to look for her son Montgomery (the posh actor Grayson Cunlick), who has gone missing after going off to write an article about a mysterious Dr Farquar. The other sailors believe that the voyage is cursed due to the stories of ships disappearing around the islands.

They come across part of another ship that had been hit by a torpedo and find two people still alive. In it is Arlen Parker (the Hollywood star Sal Klimer) and his assistant Lawton (Geno Wright). Parker claims he was following a Japanese warship when his ship was torpedoed by a German submarine.

They reach the island of Dr Farquar, played by the legendary Brandon Farlow. Dr Farquar lives in the large white house on the hill, surrounded by gruesome looking servants in uniform (think of the people you see in supermarkets) called Wokners. In a nearby village are more gormless looking creatures, called Borlock's. These seem a bit wilder and cannot speak. Farquar tells them that they all obey his every word.

Lady Ruffsnatch's son Monty is now working for Dr Farquar and refuses to leave. Arlen Parker goes out looking for Nazis and realises that something is not right with the locals. He begins to believe Dr Farquar is experimenting with humans and animals. Arlen Parker also gets close to panther woman, played by the young and attractive Lara. But he does not know she is part animal.

One evening over dinner, Parker tells Farquar that a war is coming, and that they must all get off the island. Farquar wants them to stay (so that he can get Parker to have sex with panther woman and produce a new breed of slave). Panther woman begins to fall in love with Arlen and tells him the truth: those in uniform, the Wokners, are the experiments that worked; the Borlocks are the experiments that didn't quite go to plan. There is another problem; the only time the ship will get back over the barrier reef happens soon, and then they will be stranded for months.

Farquar tells captain Rimlick he can cure his blindness, if he stays for a few more days. Rimlick agrees. Dr Farquar then gets the Wokners to kill the rest of the crew on the ship. Farquar states he is not a Nazi. In fact, he is a communist, and all communist leaders need supplicant workers to keep their empire going.

On the other side of the island, Parker gets the Borlocks to rebel. The creatures set fire to the village. The surviving members try to get to the ship. Monty tries to stop them, but is killed by his own mother, who tells the others she would never be able to show her face in Marks and Spencer's again if they found out her son was a communist. The fire spreads up to the mansion. The others reach the jetty. Arlen Parker is saved from being killed by panther woman, who dies trying to protect him. They reach the ship, and it sails away as the island burns.

#

By the time Kincaid finished the story, the sun was setting, and we were three drinks down. A film based on the book was made a few years later. It was a straightforward B movie horror, with the politics left out. After the war the film was consigned to late night television. Now it was 1996. This made it an ideal time to make a film about charismatic leaders trying to control the population with experiments and lies.

Our director, John Kurtis, was a South African who had made a few low budget horrors in the late eighties and early nineties, which had sold well in the Blockbuster video stores. He believed in the supernatural, that he had shamanic powers, and that witches and wizards really existed. He had been trying to get this production off the ground for a while. Luckily, a few things happened, which he said was fate. Dolly the cloned sheep had made headlines all around the world, and *The Island of Dr Farquars Fiends* was mentioned. When the Hollywood executives looked to see who owned the film rights, it was the strange Mr Kurtis.

At the same time, Brandon Farlow, the famous method actor who had not done anything for years, was suddenly willing to make a film whilst doing as little as possible, to pay off a massive tax bill. Kurtis managed to meet him, and Farlow agreed to be in the film, if Kurtis was the director. Hollywood knew they had to cash in before Farlow died; and that's what had brought us all here.

'I'm lucky,' said Kincaid as he made another round of drinks. 'I came up through the old British system. I must have made a hundred films in the studios at Borehamwood.'

'Strange,' dame Helen replied. 'I've always considered you to be one of the last great J. Arthur Rankers. Did you never work at Pinewood?'

Kincaid gently held her hand.

'Alas, dear lady, if only I had your many, many, many, many years of acting experience. At Pinewood I might have played Twist with your Mrs Thingummy.' He poured out the cocktails. 'Like so many other men did.'

'I only signed on for this because it's an Oscar contender,' said Dame Helen.

She was right. Even before the movie had started production there was a buzz (not the one I often heard from dame Helen's tent) about the film. Hollywood executives were coming over whilst the film was in production to give it a contender feel.

'What's it like to win an Oscar?' I asked Helen.

The grand dame of British acting, the doyen of film and theatre, the woman who had done everything from Shakespeare to Sorkin, replied with conviction.

'Absolutely fucking marvellous. A BAFTA is good, but the BBC are tighter than a duck's arse.' She opened her handbag and placed both awards on the bar. 'For good luck. Although I would have changed the title of "The Island of Dr Farquar's Fiends" to something catchier.'

Kincaid placed the award at either end of the bar.

'And what would that be, dear lady?' Reginald asked.

'Never mind the Borlocks.' With that, Dame Helen said goodnight and went back to her tent.

'My nan would be impressed that I'm in a film with Dame Helen Mivvy,' I said. 'She remembers her from the Forties.'

'When Dame Helen started acting, the Dead Sea was just ill.' Kincaid poured us out a nightcap.

I stared at that golden statuette, and knew I would do anything to win one.

Five

The next morning, I took a good look at my tent. It was bigger than my bedroom at home. I put up an old black and white picture of Brandon Farlow. Mean, moody and magnificent. I also put up a picture of Sal Klimer dressed as a sheriff from one of the film magazines, and a picture of Lara Benson, dressed in a strategically tailored football shirt from another type of magazine. Kiss, kiss, bang, bang. I went out and looked around.

The island itself wasn't that large. A former president had used it as his private retreat. When the revolution came, he only just managed to escape to a safe oil rich country and given sanctuary on humanitarian grounds; that and the hundreds of millions in aid money he had stashed away in offshore accounts. Due to the barrier reef, everything had to be bought into the by small boats.

Watching the crew offload boxes and cameras, I wondered if it would have been easier to film this in a more accessible jungle. Somewhere closer to a hotel and a port perhaps? I found out later the company that owned the island (which incidentally was run by the son of the deposed dictator) was going to build a series of luxury resorts as soon as we finished and had given the film company a massive discount to promote the island. What they didn't know was that Kurtis was going to make a black and white movie. I continued to walk around the island.

The main set was the large white colonial house on the hill. Behind that were barns that had been turned into smaller sets, equipment stores, and an editing room. Down a footpath was the film crew camp, the canteen area, and the make-up/costume area. The extras huts were further in the jungle. They were surfers and gym bunnies who were going to be turned into wild creatures.

I noticed Lara talking to a few of the extras as they went down to the beach. I followed. As one of the few young and available males on the island, and let's be honest, a future famous actor, I thought I must be like catnip to this lot. Now, with this being so early in the book, I must be coming across as a complete shit bag. It's hard to be the hero in your own story when you know you're being a bit of a bag of shit at the beginning. I can only say that as part of my character arc, I get better, I promise (with less commas).

A group of girls walked along the shore towards a luxurious yacht moored to the jetty. Perhaps it was Brandon Farlow, or Sal Klimer? Somebody on the yacht held up a bottle of champagne. It was Grayson Cunlick, the Etonian Oxbridge posh actor who had spent most of his career playing Etonian Oxbridge posh types. He wore a polo shirt with the collars up, and the sleeves of a cashmere sweater tied across his chest. Was he expecting a quick game of polo? He was also wearing green moccasins. I think they were made from the feathers of baby Parakeets. He was a few years older than me, but there was something more. Where my holidays had consisted of piss ups somewhere in the Mediterranean, Grayson probably spent his gap year exploring Thailand or skiing down some exclusive resort. Was I jealous? Of course. We were both fighting for the same amount of time in front of the camera. To be nominated for best supporting Actor it was easier if there were no other supporting actors in the film. For this holiday I had bought three pairs of boxer shorts, one of them had a wine stain. Grayson walked down the jetty, opened the gates, and came up to me.

'Hello, I've got a small travel holdall in the main cabin. Could you bring it over to the actor's camp.'
It wasn't a question. He was about to move on when Lara stopped him.

'No, this is Liam Wells. He *is* one of the actors.'
Grayson laughed, still looking at Lara. That seemed to be the end of it. No apology, no shaking hands, and Lara describing me as "one of the actors" rather than "an actor." I should have replied 'Why don't you shove that travel holdall up your

posh sticky arsehole.' But I didn't think of that reply until about twelve hours later.

Grayson and Lara walked back to the camp, and I followed behind. I couldn't keep up. The flip flops my mum had got me from Woolworths were already falling apart. Grayson was telling her about a couple of films he was thinking of doing. As an established actor he could have taken a lead role in another film, but he said he wanted to play the part of Montague because he found the character so intriguing. It was bollocks. Any film with a whisper of an Oscar nomination drew in actors quicker than a shark smelling blood.

We reached my camp. Grayson immediately knew the pecking order. Dame Helen Mivvy was the top of the British pops. Oscar winners were always welcome in Hollywood. Reginald Kincaid was next. He had been in a couple of films and shows in the sixties. The seventies consisted of a few embarrassingly very soft-core comedies, Confessions of a Doughnut Poker, or something like that. Luckily, Kincaid had become the face of a popular chocolate bar, and those series of adverts got him through the wilderness years. He had been in a few tired and emotional scenes on live television in the eighties which had hindered his career for a while; but thanks to the lad culture that now evaded the nineties he was seen as a bit of a living legend. It made him a sort of Archbishop in acting.

    Grayson was next in line when it came to being famous, if only because he was never going to starve. He could play Wilfred Owen in one film, wait a couple of years living off his family's money, then play Douglas Bader in another film. Tin hat to tin legs in one short jump. Hollywood saw him as an English slightly eccentric character. Every couple of years it was a different time period, a different version of the large house, with the rich above and the servant's downstairs. When Grayson had finished playing the dashing son, he would be next in line for the military uncle or the Lordly father figure. Tin stars to tin pots with voice overs in-between.

    Lara was the attractive young actress. The film camera loved her eyes, and teenage boys loved her knockers. It was sad that women had to debase themselves in this patriarchal society. But if I had a body like that, I would have those baps on display every day; and make sure that everyone was paying to look. Her path to fame might lay in playing a Bond girl, or a gangster's mistress. She was often described as "up and coming," meaning she was at the age when both young and old could fancy her. The last thing I wanted was for Lara and Grayson to come out of this film with tabloid rumours of romance. I was a nobody who wanted to be a somebody, and I was willing to sell my soul and my integrity to do it.

'Darling Helen,' said Grayson. 'We missed you at Bobo's Bistro off the cap this year. I had a wonderful chat about you with Tony Hopkins. He's dying to work with both of us in a Shakespeare film.'

'Titus?' Helen asked.

'He always has been,' Grayson replied. 'But I don't mind paying just to get him to order a bottle of Chianti.' He turned in the same way a TV host in a game show would. 'And dear old Reggie. I haven't seen you since the second call back on Another Country. Such a shame you didn't get it.'

'I know,' Kincaid replied. 'Especially as you had the final say.'

Grayson handed over a jar of olives. 'And I feel such a heel. But I did hear on the grapevine that you are up for Lord of the Rings. I heard Harvey Weinstein had canned it?'

'The fat pervy philistine wanted to make a single film,' Kincaid replied. 'No respect. New Line are looking to make a trilogy.'

'I've been offered a part in the same film as well,' I said, trying to get in on the act.

Grayson looked at me as if I was a turd that had been dropped onto his expensive deck shoes. 'What character. Aragorn, Legolas?'

Not having read the book, I paused. 'No. One of the hobbits.'

I was lucky. A few years ago, I had met a guy at a party. We ended up spending the night smoking pot and talking about books that should be turned into films. I said there was a book called *Trainspotting*, which said something about the chemical culture we were living in. This other guy kept going on about the *Lord of the Rings* and how it was the ultimate story of good and evil; and how the nature of random causation can sometimes end up with the same result as divine intervention. I remembered it was also the last book that one of my heroes, Bill Hicks, had read before he died. It was strange how two books that two pot heads in some shitty two bed flat above a shop had talked about were now being turned into two major films. I guess there were a lot of well-paid producers in Hollywood at the time who were doing the same drugs, just in more comfortable surroundings.

Dame Helen saved me from any further embarrassment.

'Don't be so pedantic Grayson. Lee is full of enthusiasm.' (I was going to correct her about my name, but I didn't know what pedantic meant) Helen turned to her audience. 'When one starts out acting it really is a game of chance. I remember doing local rep at the Watford Palace theatre for The Diary of Ann Frank. I got the part of the elder sister, Margot. Unfortunately, some of the other actors were so awful even the scenery groaned. One night it was so bad that when the gestapo came onto the stage, someone in the audience shouted, "She's in the loft." It made the newspapers. A film agent came to see if it was as bad as they said and landed me my first film role. I suppose the moral of the story is: never turn down anything that's got Nazi's or monsters in it. If it's good the audience will warm to you, and if it's bad they won't remember you anyway.'

I could have said something about the film we were making had a bit of both, although I soon found out that on this island nothing was what it seemed.

Six

I stayed at the bar. Grayson was telling everyone about how he had met Bono and Madonna, with the idea of working on a charity single for those suffering with prostate cancer. It was going to be a cover version of Meatloaf's "Dead Ringer for Love".

'I was once asked to do a duet with Paul McCartney,' said Dame Helen. 'People say my version of The Beatles "A Day in the Life," is absolutely haunting.'

'I'm not surprised,' said Kincaid. 'You continually murder it.'

Dame Helen ignored the comment.

'Wasn't you in the Magical Mystery Tour Reginald?'
Kincaid nodded. 'I played the walrus.'

'Well please let us know when you've stopped.'
It would seem Dame Helen she didn't miss a trick. Such a shame she couldn't remember my name. By now I was drunk from the feet up. Grayson was boring me. What I needed was some food to soak up the alcohol.

The jungle footpath was lit with small yellow fairy lights. We had been told not to leave food in the tents, as it attracted bugs, which would attract bigger creatures. So, everyone should eat in the canteen, which was a picnic area in a clearing and a couple of women in a mobile kitchen. As I staggered through the trees, I saw a cat up in the branches about to be sexually assaulted by a monkey. The poor little bastard, I thought; and believed that the only way to save it was by throwing a coconut near the monkey. I realise now that throwing coconuts in the dark whilst drunk is frowned upon. It struck the cat on the side of the head, knocking it off the branch. Fuck. But I believe I undoubtably stopped it from being molested. Unfortunately, one of the cooks did not agree.

'He kill cat. He kill cat,' she shouted. She then started speaking in what sounded like French to the other cooks. I tried to explain to the three women that I was saving the cat, to stop it being attacked by monkey.

'You monkey,' they said. 'You try kill cat.'

'No, no, no. I wanted to save cat from monkey sex, but coconut heavy.' I held my hand open as if holding a gorilla's balls.

'You want coconut monkey sex?'
Cameron, an apprentice technician, stumbled over. He listened to the women, nodded every so often, and finally spoke.

'Un demi-esprit, simple homme de cerveau de singe. il pense avoir sauvé le chat.'

The women seemed to accept this and went back to work.

'Thanks,' I said. 'Liam wells.'

'Cameron.' He shook my hand.

'Did you tell them I was having a shit?'

Cameron shook his head.

'I told them you were a bit simple. And that some of the monkeys bought over here for filming have already escaped.' I suddenly realised there was something strange about the women. 'How come all the cooks are wearing lacy underwear?'

'Oh,' said Cameron. 'They're also hookers.' He handed me a joint.

There is a universal truth that most film crews are degenerate fucks. Sex, drugs, gambling, all before breakfast. The dela was you had to hit your game when the director said "Action."

For the rest of the time, you were just there to wait.

'Where did you get this?'

'Reginald Kincaid,' said Cameron nodded. 'He knows a man in Manilla.'

'Are we near Manila?'

Cameron shrugged. I still needed food. He went to get some curry.

I picked up a marshmallow Flumps and a strawberry Lanky Larry then walked down to a line of refrigerators. The cook was watching me.

'Water?'

'Wada?' The cook looked around. 'Minkey boy want wada.' I pointed to the bottles. 'Water here?'

'No wet pussy.' She laughed.

Ah yes, who could resist the wit and humour of hookers.

Being English, I am never sure how complementary stuff works when abroad. Do I just take a bottle, do I leave a tip? In the end I took two bottles, and sat at a table, trying to pick the right moment to run away. I picked up a sachet of mayonnaise and pretended to read it. The cat came over to thank me. I love animals. My grandad used to keep rabbits. For years I thought he was setting them free. He wasn't, he was setting them in pies and pastas. We were a dog family, but I loved cats as well. As Cameron came over with the food I tried to open the sachet of mayonnaise. I drunkenly gave it a squeeze and sent an arc of creamy mayonnaise into the air, hitting the cat.

'Shit.'

The hooker's pussy was now covered in white cunk. Cameron sat down.

'Shit.

The little furry fucker ran towards the canteen. I heard one of the women cry out, and not in a good way. I decided to take my takeaway, away, and staggered towards the actor's camp. I was sure everything would be fine in the morning.

Seven

I woke up feeling as if a grumpy monkey had ambled into my tent and shat in my mouth. The air was hotter than a Mexican fart. Flies buzzed over my plate of curry. This was not the start I had wanted on my first feature film.

There was a washroom in another camp. After a shit, shave, and shower, I felt a bit better. Luckily the canteen area was busy. I avoided speaking to the hookers. Grabbing a cup of coffee and a banana, I walked down to the production area and went up to a line of blackboards. The first one had the cast for make-up times:

Brandon Farlow: Doctor Farquar.

Sal Klimer: Arlen Parker.

Helen Mivvy: Lady Ruffsnatch.

Reginald Kincaid: Captain Rimlick.

Grayson Cunlick: Montague Ruffsnatch.

Geno Wright: Walton

Lara Benson: Panther woman.

I looked for my own name. It was on the next board.

Liam Wells: Jack Bates.

It meant I probably wouldn't appear in any close ups. I only had a small part (not in the Biblical sense). My lines were what they called reactions and expos: "What's that Lassie, Timmy's fallen down the well again?" Or "Jim, you were the best dam pilot at space academy, until your mother died in a bizarre lawnmower accident that the police have never solved." What I had to do was get friendly with the director.

John Kurtis wore a Stetson, purple lensed aviator sunglasses, and a safari suit, giving the impression of a weapon loving closet homosexual on a continental holiday. He smoked using an ivory cigarette holder, allowing him to express himself with his hands. He called us over and explained that a ghost wizard had told him the film had to be made this way, I couldn't help but notice he had a strong Scottish accent.

'What's he going on about?' I asked.

'He believes in the occult,' Kincaid replied. 'A magical space wizard told him this film was going to be special. Kurtis told Brandon Farlow, who also believes in magic, and he told Hollywood, who believe in money.'

We were on a multi-million-dollar film, set in an island paradise, with actors who should have been in a rest home, all because some Glaswegian loon in a cowboy hat had a dream while off his nut. I was impressed. We walked up to the main set.

The white house was a gothic mansion. It had a large tower, a veranda, a courtyard, and a series of smaller out buildings. These would be used for the internal shots; the ships cabin, a library, the kitchen, a science laboratory in what was going to be "The House of Pain." Everything was all done in a mixture of colonial art deco and south pacific tribal patterns. The motif seemed to be strange, tattooed creatures with exaggerated lips, penises or breasts, a bit like most modern reality TV shows.

Whilst the others were busy looking around the sets, I followed Kurtis into the editing van.

'Mr Kurtis,' I said. 'I'd just like to thank you for the opportunity of being in this film.' He looked at me as if I had just farted in his hat. 'Liam Wells,' I continued. 'I was in Gringe Hall. The searing indictment of Thatcher's Britain in the late 80's. I played the boy who ends up getting addicted to heroin and is forced to do a burglary in a Pizza shop to pay back a drug debt. When he's found dead under shelves of pepperoni, mushrooms, ham, pineapple, and chillies, the police don't know if its murder, or if he'd topped himself. I thought you'd seen it?'

Kurtis shook his head.

'No. But you are definitely related to T.B. Wells, right? My Shaman said that you were the missing link.'

Here was the thing, which I might as well confess now. Somewhere in pre-production someone had said that the author of the book was my great grandfather. I could have said no, hoping that my talent would be spotted in rehearsals.

'Of course I am,' I lied.

For Kurtis that was enough. 'Good. The stars foretold that our lives would change on this island.'

I decided to use the universe to my own advantage. 'My great grandfather passed down the secret that Montague Ruffsnatch was gay. Perhaps if the actor playing him could camp it up a little?'

Kurtis pondered for a while. 'Good idea. More publicity.'

As he walked away, I allowed myself a smile. Put that in your travel bag and smoke it.

Eight

The film was going to be shot in chronologic order. The schedule was tight, but Hollywood star Brandon Farlow only agreed to film on certain days, when Jupiter was in Uranus, or something like that. Today was just going to be me, Kincaid and Dame Helen inside the wheel deck of *la Fanny Pourrie*. Costume and make-up were easy for me. Eve, the lady in charge, had everything laid out. Mine was a naval officers' jacket, white shirt and blue trousers. My only prop was a cutlass sword. Kincaid, as the immutable Captain Rimlick, wore a white cap, dirty grandad shirt, cream trousers. He also had to wear an eye patch. Dame Helen was a bit smarter than us. Knowing that this was a black and white film (the producers hoping it would give it the Schindler's List effect), she had her costumes especially made to suit the lighting. She also had her own light rig and a special lens to be used whenever the camera was on her. The old girl was right; there are no large or small parts, you just need to shine with the time you've got. The fog machine was turned on. Take One.

#

Kincaid and Dame Helen stood looking out at the fog as I rushed into the wheel room.

Kincaid: 'Is that you, young Jack Bates?' (The trick is to get the names in within the first few minutes.)

Me: 'Yes, captain Rimlick (see). How did you know which cabin I was in?'

The half blind (and half cut) captain held out his hand and touched my face.

Kincaid: 'Whilst everyone was asleep, I went down into the galley and felt your knob. There is a scratch in the brass where the door must have hit something. Don't wake the others, but my sight is getting worse, and in these treacherous waters the old girl could go down on me at any minute.' (I looked at lady Ruffsnatch.) 'Now young master Bates,' continued the captain. 'You must take the wheel. I'm afraid my old one eye has gone to the dogs, and Lady Ruffsnatch has paid us good money to find her son, believed to be shipwrecked among these unknown islands.' (That's called exposition, giving a back of backstory to the audience.)

   I steered through the mist using the small porcelain Charlie Chaplin figurine on the window as a guide to know where the front of the ship was (also helps the audience know its set in the past). In the mist came the faint sound of clanging.

Kincaid: 'Is that your bell end, young Jack?'

Me: 'No captain. It must be another ship, but my eyesight is as bad as yours.'

Kincaid took a sip of whiskey: 'I told you not to do it every night boy.'

Me: 'Starboard bow. It's part of a ship.'

That was when we would cut to the hero Sal Klimer, as Arlen Parker, and his black assistant Lawton (Geno Wright) as they floated in the ocean on a piece of ship. They would then climb up a ladder and give their names and a bit more exposition.

Dame Helen: 'Have you seen my little Monty?'

Kincaid: 'Certainly not. I was merely checking the keyhole to make sure it was working properly.'

Me: 'She means her son, captain.'

At this point Klimer would tell us they had been following a Japanese warship when their ship was torpedoed by a Nazi submarine. We are shocked. This was 1936, and the thought of another war seemed more fiction than fact. Stuff like this is always great. It the bit where the audience knows what's going to happen next, but we have no idea. I then call out (a good bit for me, as the camera would have only me in the shot).

Me: 'Captain. A light.'

Through the mist a small light appeared high up on a hill. Klimer would assume control. He would check a map and say there should not be an island there, just a treacherous barrier reef. He would then steer us towards the light, with the bottom of the ship crunching over the rocks. We make it through the mist and see the shadow of a deserted island. We dock on a long wooden jetty. The other sailors refuse to help, believing the island is cursed, and that we should never get off the boat. But Parker is the hero. And so, we head towards the light on the island of Dr Farquar, not knowing there are beastlike eyes watching us from the jungle.

Nine

Down on the farm its ride, ride, ride.

Indians in Moscow, Jack Pelter and his sex change chicken.

We had the first scenes in the can. John Kurtis seemed happy. Lara sat by the fire as Grayson Cunlick called us into the camp as if he owned the place.

'Reggie. Dame Helen,' Grayson called out. 'Allow me to fix you a drink. I've bought my own. It's a 53 Margaux. A lot older than you, but just as cheeky.'

God, I hated the man. He then gave an oily smile to the director.

'John. I've also got a bottle of Green Spot from my boat.' Kurtis ignored him and turned to me.

'Thanks for today,' he said. 'The camera liked you. I may get you to do a few of Sal Klimer's stand ins.' He walked away.

I glanced at Lara. The director had spoken to me. When they say power is a great aphrodisiac, it's true. Grayson turned to Lara.

'Would you like to come up to my yacht and see my fax machine?'

Lara shook her head. 'No, thanks. I've got an early day in make up tomorrow. Liam, could you walk me to my tent?'

I couldn't help but smile. Well, well, well. Who was King shit now?

The trip to the tent was short and sweet. I noticed she was wearing a brown choker, a sand-coloured crop top, and brown stretch shorts. She looked like a cat already.

'What's he like?' Lara asked.

'I can't stand those posh wankers,' I said. 'He will never know what it means to choose between acting or getting a job just to pay the bills.' I gave my best line. 'He's Blur, I'm oasis.'

Lara shook her head. 'Not Grayson. I'm not going to be his beard.'

I had no idea what she was talking about.

'I meant John Kurtis,' she said as she opened her tent. 'What did you think about him?'

To be honest, I was thinking more about getting into her flaps than under the cowboy hat of a Scottish Growler. 'He's good,' was my reply. 'He's doing it by the book.'

'He doesn't like improvisation?'

'No, I mean he's got a book of spells. He checks his chakras every morning.'

'My old P.E teacher used to do the same.' Lara said. 'He's not allowed to use computers now.' With that she decided she

needed to change her game plan. 'I suppose I'd better get my head down then. Goodnight.'
With that she went into her tent.

Bugger. I went back to my camp. Kincaid handed me a martini.

'Been a bit premature? You would be better off just focusing on your part, dear boy.'

'I was hoping to do that in Lara's tent.'
Kincaid shook his head. 'The best bit of professional advice I can give you is, get the work done first. There are a lot of people relying on you.' The salubrious socialist handed me a ready rolled joint.
I sat at the makeshift bar and took a deep hit.

'Where are you getting all this stuff from?'
He smiled. 'Just because one is a trained actor, one should never feel as though they have been reduced to the status as a bum.' He poured another drink. 'If I can give you another bit of advice, if you must do any of Sal Klimer's stand ins, don't act. Don't pretend to be Sal Klimer playing the character of Arlen Parker. Just be you.'
No shit, Sherlock. 'Don't worry,' I said. 'I'm a professional.'
I then proceeded to drink my martini and smoke my joint, whilst all the time wondering what Lara Benson was doing in her tent.

Dame Helen came over and polished her BAFTA.

'Swapsies?' I passed her the joint, and she handed me the Oscar to clean.

'Had my first one from Humphrey Bogart himself,' she said as she took a big hit.

Dame Helen and Kincaid then spent the next hour exchanging in verbal Top Trumps of famous people, with Helen holding most of the joint, and Kincaid farting every time he moved. Dame Helen said that cannabis was freely available when Shakespeare was alive. No wonder some of his plays contained men being turned into donkeys and people changing genders on a magical island. He was clearly smoking the good stuff.

It had been a good day. A couple of scenes in the bag, and I was hob knobbing with the big players. I hoped that one day someone would be standing there talking about the time they met me.

Ten

Being such a small cast, some of us were asked to be extras in the crowd scenes containing Borlocks and the Wokners. The Borlocks were just large dumb creatures. Because it wasn't a speaking part, they could put me in a cheap looking gorilla costume, place me in the background and not worry too much how I looked between a pair of old Borlocks. I joined Cameron, who was also in a gorilla costume. Even with a mask I could see he was completely stoned.
Dexter, the assistant director, called our group over.

'I want some of you to make the sound of a small simian.' Cameron, who was stood behind me, began to sing.

'You can call me Al,'

'No,' said Dexter. 'That's a Paul Simon. I want you to make noises like monkeys, and the others to clap as sending messages.'

When he walked away, Cameron lit a joint.

'I think they were selling these costumes in Woolworths?' He stood against a tree and scratched his back. 'We should have been Wokners. I bet they are getting all the pussy.'

We walked towards the village. Those Borlocks who were going to be in the foreground had teeth missing, hairy nipples, and pot bellies. It was like grab a granny night in Burnley. When I looked over at the Wokners they were all a bit fitter. The males had trousers, jackets, and boots, and most of them had just come from the gym. The female Wokners wore tight dresses and leather boots. It was a cross between the Playboy mansion and London Zoo. I followed Cameron and the rest of the Borlocks to the edge of the jungle. Cameron kept smoking his joint. It would be another half an hour before everyone had been placed on their marks.

'I'd love to give that milf Eve in the costume hut a good seeing to,' he said. 'I bet she is absolutely groaning for it. At her age it's probably like a clown's pocket, so I would probably do her doggy style so I could finish on her back.'

'You are a silver-tongued poet.'

Cameron continued to smoke his joint.

I noticed that a lot of the film crew had been dressed up as extras, and most of them appeared to be getting stoned. As Dexter got the main characters into place, I saw Lara. Being a stand in meant getting the camera and the lighting in the correct position without bothering the star. If it was a two shot, where two people were talking, the first character would be filmed speaking, I would say Klimer's out of shot, and then the camera would film the first character's reaction. All

Klimer had to do was be filmed saying his lines, and in the edit the film would look like both people were speaking to each other. He had a couple of scenes with Lara.

#

Once the scene had been done, I went back to costume to get changed. As I headed back to camp I saw Lara wading into the sea. She was probably just going to stand up to her waist in the water and take a really long piss. She looked great in a bikini. Those legs were longer than my life span prediction. I always thought I was a breast man, but Jesus, that arse. You could have slipped a rusty coin down there, and ten steps later it would come out a polished sovereign. Nowadays everyone talks about different genders like they are choosing a sofa. I don't mind what you are into; but I love being a man. Even the smell of women turns me on. And I know that everyone has a bum, including me, and if you want to go sniffing around there after curry night then hats off to you; but there was something about the way each of her buttocks moved like God's bowling balls as she tried to tiptoe above each wave. She turned as the sea rolled above her soft yet taut stomach and called me to join her.

This is it. This is it. I hoped she would turn around again, so I could give my willy a quick tug, just to stretch it out a bit so you could at least see something in my shorts. I also hoped the water wasn't too cold. I hung my shirt on a tree, pulled the choirboys breakfast a few times, and gave myself the final once over to make sure it didn't look like I had a wet penny in my pocket.

I went into the sea. Birds flew over the waves. Fish swam in the shallows. My willy shrivelled to the size of a wrinkled acorn. I let the next wave drag me closer. I wanted to sound like Grayson, the sort of guy who went on a couple of holidays a year just because he could.

'I should have brought my snorkelling gear,' I said to her. 'I love diving just as much as acting.'
Lara agreed.

'When did you last do your PADI?'
All I had to do was stay cool. 'At a casting call for the younger brother in My Left Foot.' I replied. I gave it my best Irish impression. 'Oh begorrah, I can't go to mass again just wearing the right shoe.'
Lara laughed. A wave moved us closer.

'What that?' she asked.

'Sorry.' I took a step back.

I heard what sounded like the echo of a giant film projector with its reels turning. Spots appeared in the sky. They grew bigger. It was a fleet of helicopters heading towards us. The sound of the blades was a bittersweet symphony as they flew in and alongside the palm trees. They were a mixture of new and old army choppers. Two of them were carrying large silver American style trailers. Hollywood had arrived.

Eleven

The helicopters went to the side of the island where the trees had been cleared, and a fence put up. This was where the Hollywood stars would be staying. We got our stuff and walked over as the helicopters placed the two large silver nineteen fifties style trailers down. A Hollywood executive in a suit called out to us.

'Mr Farlow is very concerned about protecting the environment.'

Another helicopter landed further away. Two golf carts appeared (where was all this shit coming from?). Brandon Farlow was helped out of the helicopter. Christ, he was a lump. He had been a big star in the fifties and sixties. Now, he was just big. The golf cart almost buckled when he got in it. It drove up the to where a host of executives were waiting. As soon as it stopped, they were on him like ticks on a donkey's nob. Farlow looked around, spoke to one of them, and went into his trailer. One Hollywood executive came over to us.

'Is there an electrician here?'

Cameron raised his hand. The executive gave an order.

'Mr Farlow is hot. You must turn the temperature down.'

Cameron looked at him. 'The whole island?'

The executive wanted the matter solved quickly. 'Put some air conditioning units under the trailer. Get it done in the next ten minutes.' The executive saw Kincaid and gave a big smile. 'Reginald Kincaid. Mr Farlow remembers you from the chocolate bar adverts twenty years ago and hopes to have a great working relationship with you.' The executive then turned to Helen. 'Dame Helen Mivvy. What an honour. And I believe Mr Farlow has come across your face before.'

'I was young and struggling for work at the time,' Helen replied.

The executive pulled out a sheet of paper. 'Mr Farlow always likes to work with old friends. If you could just sign here. It's a declaration that you will not speak or even look at Mr Farlow unless he grants permission, or speak to the press about him unless it has been written by me. Now, Mr Farlow will be delighted to see you all on set tomorrow morning, once he's had time to go through the script changes with the director.'

Helen pointed at the other golf cart now making its way up the field.

'Is that Mr Klimer. He seems to either be gesturing as us, or felching the invisible man.'

'Shit. He was due for another two hours.' The executive ran back to join the others as the golf cart stopped at the other trailer.

Sal Klimer already had a reputation of being an arrogant arsehole, on and off set. His latest film, *Owlman Returns*, a dreadful adaptation of a comic book, was destined to a big financial hit around the world. But Klimer was here because he wanted awards as well. He needed to be in a film that was whispered to be a Hollywood contender. And he needed to work with Farlow before the old fart passed away; because it would mean his name would be linked to a legend. The good news for Klimer was that neither of these things had any impact on having to treat people with respect or kindness.

As soon as he got out of the golf cart, he argued with the rest of the Hollywood executives and kept pointing at the helicopters. Evidently, he had demanded that both his and Farlow's helicopters land at the same time. It was pointed out that because of the extra weight, Farlow's helicopter had to land first, otherwise it would have run out of fuel.

Klimer went straight into his trailer, which was identical to Farlow's, then quickly called for one of the executives. A few moments later another executive appeared with a tape measure. He measured the length of Klimer's trailer and then sneaked across and measured Farlow's. He went inside, and after a few more moments he came out with a smile on his face.

This soon disappeared when Farlow's trailer door opened, and the executive went in to see him. A few moments later the executive with the tape measure was called in. This time he measured the width of Farlow's trailer and then sneaked over and measured the width of Klimer's trailer. He went inside to tell Farlow. A few moments later he came out. Before anyone could stop him, he ran down the field towards the last helicopter and hung on to the landing skids as it took off.

'We have entered a fool's paradise,' said Kincaid. 'No empire can have two kings.'

Kincaid was carrying an ice bucket with a half-finished bottle of champagne, which he used to shove the Hollywood executives out of the way. I followed. Kincaid knocked on Farlow's door and then went in without waiting for an answer. Fuck it. I followed.

Brandon Farlow sat in the corner, half bald, half his face dripping with sweat; the half-darkness cast a shadow across his face. This was one of the greatest actors that ever lived. The man who changed the movie industry for ever. I will never forget those first momentous words he spoke to us.

'You brought a bucket of fried chicken?'

'Darling Brandon. Its Reginald Kincaid. I haven't seen you since I auditioned for Last Tango in Paris. I was going to play Alan Retentive, the deliveryman who came in with the pack of butter. How have you been?'

Brandon Farlow pointed a stubby finger.

'The guy from the chocolate bar adverts in the seventies?' Kincaid nodded. 'Your wife will love something thick and brown in her mouth.'

'Did you get boxes of them as part of a royalties deal?'

'Yes,' said Kincaid. 'I used to swap down the local youth club for cannabis resin.'

Farlow sighed. 'Some people have all the luck.' The chubby man looked at me like a was a delivery boy who promised to bring him ice cream. Then he remembered something. 'I've seen you before?' Perhaps I reminded him of a waiter at an all you can eat buffet? Then Farlow got it. 'You were the shepherd boy in the kebab flavour Pot Noodle advert. Do you get any for free?'

I nodded and said the company logo. 'Boil up a bit of an animal. I dint know it was sold in America?'

'I like to know what's going on in culinary drama. Can you get some?'

I nodded again. 'I could try.'

He got out of his specially made chair. The man who had won two Oscars, had slept with hundreds of women, created thousands of dreams, and must have eaten a million double chocolate chip muffins, put his arm around me.

'What's your name again?'

'Liam wells.'

'Liam. I also like the Dirty Sanchez flavour. Have the crates sent to my trailer, and we could get along very well.' He took out the bottle of champagne from the bucket and placed some ice on his genitals. 'You know, I think this could be the beginning of a beautiful friendship.'

I remained sitting as the melted water dribbled down his chubby thighs, the executive came in. Farlow groaned, his genitals next to my face.

'Tate. Look after young Liam. He is important to me.' Tate looked at me. I felt like I had entered the Hollywood bowl, and I didn't care that it was filled with walnuts.

Once outside, I realised I was back in the world of reality.

'How am I going to get Pot Noodles in the middle of nowhere?'

'This is a film set, dear boy,' said Kincaid. 'Something will turn up.' He took out a piece of paper and wrote down a few words.

Another door opened. Sal Klimer called us over. We were both deemed to be allowed into his trailer.

'What did he say about me?'

'He's worried,' said Kincaid. 'One of the greatest actors of his generation, working with one of the greatest actors of the next generation; and that your trailer might be slightly higher off the ground than his.'

Klimer seemed impressed. Reginald Kincaid produced a piece of paper. 'Could I bother you for just a second. I have a nephew; loves you as Owlman. Just an autograph. I know it's a terrible imbroglio, but if you put your name on the dotted line I shall be on my way.'

Klimer duly signed the paper. We left as Klimer called Tate over and demanded to know the height of the trailers.

On the way back, Kincaid told me most of the executives on the island were here to make Farlow happy. He had power but no money. If he walked off the set, everyone would drown. It sounds terrible, but I wondered how to get Grayson Cunlick less scenes. With a few more lines given to me, I might even be up for Best Supporting Actor. The dream was being set in motion. It took me a while to realise Kincaid was still talking. He told me I shouldn't try to be like Brandon Farlow as he is now, being old and overweight would happen naturally. Rather, I should use the films that Farlow had starred in when he was younger and create my own method. I agreed. I was going to be mean, moody, and magnificent.

Twelve

Today was the big entrance for Brandon Farlow as Dr Farquar, and for Sal Klimer as Arlen Parker. Kincaid had told me not to indulge myself with carnal activities before filming. I took his advice and had a wank instead. I thought he meant not to go to a circus.

The beach was packed. Filming in black and white in daylight meant you had to worry about shadows, background continuity, and the heat. Everyone was on edge. Even my fake sweat was sweating. I was one of the minor characters in an ensemble cast scene. I had made my mind up to do a "McQueen," named after the legend that was Steve McQueen: if someone else was talking, you drew the camera (and the audience) towards you by lifting your hat, checking bullets, peeling an orange, doing anything to make the audience notice you. My McQueen was going to be to bite my fingernails and giving me a little quirk that I could use throughout the film. Klimer had decided that Arlen Parker needed a sort of Clark Gable moustache; but he couldn't be arsed to grow one. Instead, he had two separate hair pieces that had to be glued on every time Klimer was on set. It also meant he could stroke it when anyone else was talking. And the clapperboard went down.

#

A group of us were going to walk onto the beach and look for any survivors. That was the script. Arlen Parker walked down the pier first (he was the hero, after all). His moustache looked magnificent. As we walked behind him, I stepped on a strange white squashy blob.
Me: 'Captain Rimlick. I don't think we're alone.'
Kincaid: 'Seamen?'
Me: Looking down at the blob. 'No, I think it's just a jellyfish.' As I stare at the jellyfish, a large eye appears on the top and blinks.

Figures move among the palm trees. They have two legs, but drag themselves in a self-entitled sullen manner, like a teenager who has been asked to tidy the kitchen.
At this point I should remind you that this is 1996, and we are making a film set in 1936. Times have changed. Having a black actor play a servant role now seems slightly strange.
Wright: 'I don't like this, boss.'
Klimer, being the hero, and having a moustache, keeps going forward.

We finally get a shot of the creatures among the trees. They seem more beast than human. Grotesque ghastly wretches devoid of humanity. They hissed, groaned, and clapped as they shuffled towards us. Dame Mivvy, dressed as Lady Ruffsnatch in full Victorian style dress, pulls out a white lace handkerchief (that's the difference between a pro and an amateur).

Dame Mivvy: 'Are you sure we haven't landed at Margate?'

The sound of a horn came from somewhere on the island. All the creatures stopped. A man appeared on the beach.

'Umbala, Shaka Khan, jumbala.' It was Grayson, dressed as Montague Ruffsnatch, in straw fedora, white suit, and walking stick. He called into the trees. 'Tikama Cha. Snooka loopy, pita pan.' The creatures disappeared. Grayson came towards Klimer.

Grayson: 'Who are you, and how did you get here?'

Klimer: 'I'm Arlen Parker. I'm a floater from a big wet ship.'

Dame Mivvy: 'Monty.'

Grayson walks forward, with a distinct limp.

Grayson: 'Mother.'

Neither hug.

New figures appear. They wear uniforms and look slightly more human. Among them are panther women. Even though it was meant to be 1936, they were all dressed to arouse a 1990's audience. Lara steps forward, and stares at Klimer. There is a quick bit of exposition as Grayson explains how he ended up here. Reginald Kincaid, forever the old pro, pulls out a half-smoked cigar and moves it around his mouth, while Klimer strokes his moustache, Dame Mivvy wipes her brow with her handkerchief, and I bite my nails (it took me a while to realise that Lara was breathing deeply and letting her chest steal the scene).

We all stop as a horn blew again. A procession of creatures moved along the beach. It was Brandon dressed as Dr Farquar. He was being carried in a large wooden highchair. He wore a white sheet, white sun hat, and his face was covered in white cream. Standing behind him was a dwarf, dressed exactly the same (at this point I should say I know that many of you are thinking of Austin Powers or *Fantasy Island*, but the book came first, and I am aware that times have changed, and we are far more respectable now). We all got into position. Brandon took out a large orange and stared at it (the midget took out a satsuma)

Brandon: 'I am Dr Farquar. (points to midget) This is my son, Diddly. I'm afraid you must leave my island on the next high tide (begins to peel orange).'

Kincaid (taking out cigar): 'I've got to check the undercarriage of the old rust bucket first.'

Dame Mivvy (waving handkerchief): He's talking about the ship.'

Klimer (stroking moustache): And I need enough provisions to get to Constantinople.'

Brandon (peeling orange): 'There is an American naval base in Siam.'

Klimer: No, it must be Constantinople. On that I am adamant.'

Brandon bends down to speak to his son: 'Is that far, Diddly Farquar?' (they speak in whispers) 'Very well. You can stay until the ship is ready. But do not leave the compound. The jungle is massive. Diddly, blow the horn of Diabolos.' Diddly held up a pink conch and blew it. The chair was lifted, and we followed Dr Farquar down a path that he had created.

The uniformed creatures seemed to murmur between themselves whenever they heard clapping and screeching among the trees. As we walked, I chewed my fingernails, Kincaid played with his cigar, Klimer stroked his moustache, Grayson limped, Dame Mivvy dabbed her face with a handkerchief, and Lara breathed as if she had just finished having sex. Only Geno Wright didn't have a McQueen.

This was all gripping stuff; I can assure you. Those who have seen the film may have already noticed the glaring plot holes. Looking back, I can only say that I have seen what Disney did to Star Wars. They had millions of dollars to get things right and they still fucked up; so, I don't think we did too bad. Swipe to a large white painted southern style gothic mansion on a hill. Uniformed creatures patrolled the fence. The next scene was in the elaborately furnished dining room.

Thirteen

As we finished our soup, Brandon took out another orange.
Brandon: 'Such a shame I cannot get the radio to work. Are you really believe another war is coming?'
Klimer: 'Only America can stop them.'
At this point, Dame Mivvy let out a small but noticeable fart.
Brandon: 'Thank you for that witty retort, lady Ruffsnatch. But when you say America should be in charge of the world, should it also stop progress.'
Klimer: 'It's about keeping the world free.'
Brandon glances at Geno Wright. In the original book, the black character didn't make it to the dinner table. The director thought this little change in point of view was quite good.
Klimer: 'If the Japanese, Germans, or Communists were in charge, they would soon become dictators in their own little empire.'
Another change in POV, this time at Brandon, who had created his own little empire.

Brandon: You may be right. I think that anyone who believes that violence is the answer to social problems should be taken outside and shot. But progress is bittersweet (he kept peeling the orange). Sometimes there has to be a struggle for beauty to come out. I cannot leave here until my work is done.'

Dame Mivvy: 'And I will not leave without my boy.' She dabs her face with the white hanky. 'Please come back darling, even if it's just for the dogs. Hartley and Beaumont the pet dogs have missed licking my little Monty.' Another dab. 'And your father is in hospital. I'm afraid its terminus.'

Grayson: 'I think you mean…terminal.'

Dame Mivvy. 'No, he was knocked down outside the bus depot.'

The next course arrived.

Dame Mivvy: 'An interesting menu Dr Farquar. What is it?'

Brandon: 'Pech a la grenouille.'

Dame Mivvy: 'And do you get it delivered?' When Brandon nods, she continues. 'And what is it you do here, exactly?'

As Brandon fingered his earpiece, I realised someone was feeding his lines.

Brnadon: 'I came here with the hope of using the South American Cane Toad as a way of controlling the penile weevils on the island. I soon discovered that by merging the toad with the Candiru fish I could create the ultimate predator, the tadpole of death. I then realised the natives on the island were extremely simple. So, I carried out a series of experiments. Those who became better I called Wokners, who you see here in uniform. And those who didn't work are the Borlocks. Those things you saw in the trees. They are a rougher, more animalistic breed.'
Dame Mivvy: 'And where do you keep your Borlocks?'
Brandon: 'In my pocket. Though it can sometimes get a bit hairy. We must control them with a serum every few days.'

It was then Lara the panther woman came into the room. She was wearing a chiffon dress and some flowers in her hair (don't forget, this is pre-Game of Thrones and is set in 1936). She sat opposite Klimer and licked her lips as he stroked his moustache.
Dame Mivvy: 'I would very much like to see your Borlocks, Dr Farquar.'
Brandon places a napkin on his lap: 'Perhaps after lunch.'
Klimer (looking at Lara): 'I would like to see everything.'
Kincaid: 'Including the bush?'

Brandon finished his orange: 'I would advise you to look out for the Growler, Mr Parker. It's a creature that lives somewhere in the jungle. It almost caught my little Diddler.'

I see the midget staring at me and wonder what I have done wrong.

#

I was getting through my scenes quite quickly. I had thought about bringing some books to read, but as I barely had space for two pairs of pants, all I had was a magazine. I saw Lara reading *Bridget Jones Diary*.

'Any good?' I asked.

'It's a bit like Pride and Prejudice,' she replied. 'I would go for an audition if they turned it into a film.'

This may have been a test for me to say that she was far too attractive to be Bridget Jones, but I hadn't read the book. There had been a tv series of Pride and Prejudice last year. I didn't watch it because I thought it would be horse shit; but I remember a lot of girls at one audition all saying how great Colin Firth was walking out of a pond. Fuck me. If that's all it took to get famous, I should have taken swimming lessons rather than acting ones. I had to give an answer which made me look cultured.

'Perhaps the film could have Colin Firth walking out of a lake.' And there, dear readers, is what they call poetic irony (Spoiler alert: Colin Firth has an average sized penis). Colin Firth would later star in Bridget Jones, and there is a water scene. None of this seemed to work on Lara, who went back to reading her book.

I went to Kincaid's bar. He made me a drink and we headed along the beach until we found a spot to watch the little boats come up to the jetty. Kincaid took out an extremely large joint.

'The Borehamwood boner.' He felt the weight of the pendular beast in his hand. 'So called because it is shaped like a bone, and I invented it when I visited Stanley Kubrick in Borehamwood.' He lit it and inhaled. 'Have you ever seen the magnificent film, *2001 A Space Odyssey*?'

'No. What's it about?'

'I haven't got a fucking clue,' Kincaid replied. 'I asked Stanley, but he didn't have a fucking clue either. But it was his vision, and that's what makes a great director.' He handed me his boner. 'The problem with this film is there is more than one person in charge. Kurtis can't control Farlow, Klimer, the Hollywood executives, and be the director at the same time.' He turned to me. 'When you're on set, act like the character, don't be like Farlow and Klimer and act like a cunt. You won't have any fingernails left by next week.'

At that moment a shooting star appeared. It was probably a new satellite gushing porn and sport into millions of homes, but I still made a wish. I'm afraid to say that I wasn't really listening to Reg. With a big boner in my mouth, I put my headphones on, set my portable CD player for track twelve, and listened to Champagne Supernova at full volume. This was my one chance to be famous. I secretly wanted to be just like Farlow and Klimer and have my name up in lights as well.

Fourteen

It's chance, I tell you,' he interrupted, ' as everything is in a man's life.

    H.G. Wells, The Island of Dr. Moreau.

At that moment half a world away, pile of letters dropped onto the desk of Chief Inspector Jerry Bastad.

'The chief constable wants to see you,' said a young female officer.

Chief Inspector Bastad looked up and tapped the top of his shoulder with two fingers. The young lady knew what it meant.

'He wants to see you…sir.'

'Always obey the rank, constable. Where?' Bastad asked.

'In the car park,' the lady replied. 'Sir.' She turned and walked out of the office. As she did so, she secretly raised her own two fingers in tribute to the biggest Ranker in the police.

Chief Constable Sutcliffe stood in the car park holding an envelope. The big crowns on his shoulders denoted he was in charge. Bastad knew that everyone in the building would be looking out of the window. He gave his stiffest salute, letting the onlookers know how to do it professionally.

'Bastad,' said Sutcliffe. 'As you know, here in the police we like to reward inefficacy and incompetence with a promotion. After you had spent one shift checking every single vehicle in the headquarters car park, including my own, and issuing tickets, one of the things you were required to do was improve your relationship with your fellow colleagues. And I suggested you do some traffic duty.' Sutcliffe nodded towards the back of a police camera van. 'Do you remember taking out this particular vehicle?'

Bastad looked.

'That is correct sir. Was there something wrong with the camera?'

Chief constable Sutcliffe walked around to the front of the van. Bastad followed. As far as he could see there were no dents or scratches. Sutcliffe spoke as if giving evidence. 'I want you to cast your mind back. You were stationary at the junction between Station Road and Church Street. The weather was clear, and there was nothing obstructing your view. Did anything happen?'

Bastad tried to think, then remembered.

'There was a little shit, I mean a young lad, who said he wanted to join the police. I'm sure he was in a car that sped past a couple of times. He was a spineless looking scrote. A sneaky little turd nugget whose mother conceived him after a few rum and cokes in some grotty pub and then let some greasy council estate oik spit roast her in the car park whilst she noshed off a registered sex offender who worked in the kebab shop.' Bastad stopped. It wasn't your son, was it, sir?'

'No,' said Sutcliffe. 'It wasn't.' He handed over the envelope. 'Eight speeding tickets for the same vehicle. Eight summonses to appear at the local Magistrates Court. If found guilty, a fine of two thousand pounds, twenty-four points, and banned from driving for twenty years.'

'Good. I hope the scumbag feels the full force of the law.' Bastad looked at the papers. The summons was addressed to Chief Constable Sutcliffe.

'You were driving the car?'

Sutcliffe shook his head. 'No, you pillock. The summons are for you.'

Bastad checked every summons. They all contained blurred black and white images of possibly two people in a silver car. At first, Bastad did not understand what this had to do with him. The driver was wearing sunglasses. passenger looked like the lad that spoke to him earlier. Maybe the car was stolen, should be easy enough to check, just take the details... and...Foxtrot, Uniform...and then he saw it. The little fuckers. The police camera van in the police car park had no front registration plate. He ran around to the back of the vehicle he had signed out. The front registration on the Ford Escort in the photographs was the same as the back of the police camera van. The passenger must have deliberately distracted him by asking about joining the police, whilst his mate nicked the number plate and stuck it to his own car before he went past the speed camera.

'I can explain,' said Bastad. 'The little bastards stole police property, then sped past me eight times to get you into trouble. Don't worry, I'll find them.'
Sutcliffe shook his head.

'You signed out the van, therefore you are the one in possession and control of it. All the tickets are yours. If this gets to court you will be stuck on for dereliction of police duty, failure to look after police property, and driving a vehicle on a public highway that is not displaying the correct registration plate. I suggest you find the culprits and get them to confess, otherwise you may find yourself losing more than just your licence.'

Sutcliffe walked away, leaving Bastad to salute alone. Oh yes, he would find the little shits, and get them into court, even if he had to travel to the ends of the earth to do it. He looked up at the windows of police headquarters. Everyone, including the cleaners, all knew, and they all saluted back.

Fifteen

The Hollywood executives decided to organise a little party. British film crews had a wonderful solidarity with Jesus, in that wine was always better than water, and neither worked on Sundays. But they had eventually agreed to some hours on a Sunday to catch up with a production schedule that was slipping further and further behind, for triple time. This party was an informal way of trying to bring everyone closer together: a bit like having a "Forgive and Forget" hog roast on the Gaza strip. John Kurtis was wheeled around by a series of executives who all seemed desperate to tell him how important their jobs were. The weird thing is, even after all this time, I'm still not sure what a lot of them did.

Ironically, we were told that Farlow and Klimer would not be speaking to anyone, in order to save their voices. Another point: Klimer would only allow to have his picture taken on cameras made in the 1930's. He wouldn't eat any processed food, would allow no modern technology in his trailer, and only read papers from 1936. He walked through the party in his safari suit, stroking his moustache. Some people seemed to think that the world was a stage even when they weren't acting. The crew didn't seem to care. They were going through the alcohol at a heroic rate. Most of them would also wander into the jungle and smoke something, before coming back with a smile on their faces.

I watched Brandon Farlow as he sat on his highchair eating chicken wings. For some reason he would now only communicate through Diddly, who now had a miniature Segway, and moved backwards and forwards between Farlow and whatever member of staff who wanted to tell him how great he was.

I kept looking around, hoping to find Lara. Geno Wright came over.

'I heard you're related to the writer of the original story?'

'Yes,' I lied. Then knew I had to say something else. 'My great grandfather may have written the book, but the publishing company made all the money.'

Geno seemed to know the feeling. 'Have you got anything lined up after this?'

'My agent mentioned some film about train spotters, and some other film about a lord and his ring.'

'My agent wants me to be the next Will Smith.' Geno shook his head. 'But I didn't grow up Bel Air.'

The theme tune came into my head. I wondered where Geno was born and raised.

Geno continued. 'After this I've got a pimp, a gangster, and a slave; and all three of them are riding on this one being a hit. How do you think this film is going?'

'Pretty good,' I lied, again. I had become the Forest Gump of lying. Lie, Liam, lie.

Geno shook his head. 'It's not. Brandon can't be bothered to learn his lines, and Klimer keeps trying to direct the director. I speak to the camera crew every morning. The bosses have paid Brandon up front. That's why we are doing it in order. If he dies before it's over, Grayson will take his place as the main antagonist.'

That was a bit of a kicker. I could see Kurtis being harangued by executives. He was now drinking Jack Daniels straight from the bottle; and as soon as he put one cigarette out, he lit up another. I had to speak to him about making sure Grayson didn't get any more lines. My ambition was thwarted somewhat by seeing Lara and Grayson join Kurtis and a few executives. I took another Pina Colada and made my way over.

Grayson ignored me. It was only when Lara got a chance to speak that I was finally introduced.

'Grayson was just telling us how the original Moon parties were based on religious festivals, and how the natives would see them as spiritual encounters with creatures from the jungle and the sea. Did your great grandfather take part in any rituals?'

Grayson laughed.

'I hope I didn't sound too condescending.' He turned to me. 'The word "condescending" means talking down to people as you try to explain something to them.'

I finished my drink in three gulps, and replied, 'What does the word "Cunt" mean?'

It would appear I had found my social level, and it wasn't with this crowd. Although I did see Kurtis smile. I left to get another Pina Colada, Lara joined me.

'You're quite the bad boy, aren't you?'

I found out later she had heard the executives didn't like Grayson. He was rich, and could give up acting at any time, and so couldn't be controlled. That night I didn't care. We mingled, as they say is all the right circles. She had chosen me over Grayson. I suppose I was loud young man that night; but there are times when you feel so invincible that you believe you can do anything you want. At the end of the night, we all walked back to the actor's camp using the glow of yellow footlights. Lara held my hand after allegedly seeing a monkey in a tree having a wank.

Sixteen

'I'm a professional John; I can rise above it. But look. When I stand on this side of the table to stare at the map, its upside down.' Sal Klimer looked at the director. 'My character Arlen Parker trained to be a spy in Washington, but he never learned to read maps upside down.'

'Are you sure?' John Kurtis asked him. 'I've read the book and written the script, and at no point has anyone mentioned anything about a fictional character going to spy school.'

'Of course I did,' Klimer replied. 'I've set out his whole career.' Klimer held out a piece of paper. 'Look at the dates John. March 1934 to September 1935. Spy training school, including a week's break to go visit the Hoover Dam being built. I had classes every day. How to send a secret message by pigeon; how to wear a trench coat, how to slap a man so that he takes it and likes it. Do you see anything in there about reading a map upside down John? Do you?'

John Kurtis sighed.

'It's quite simple Sal.'

'Arlen.'

'Sorry, Arlen. It's quite simple.' At this point Kurtis moved from behind the camera and walked forward.

'Whoa, whoa, whoa, sweet child of mine' said Klimer. 'Where the fuck are you going?' He pointed at the floor around him. 'Here is my temple. This is where I create the magic that has made me one of the highest paid movie stars in the world. I am doing you a great fucking favour just by being here. So, from now on, don't ever walk on to my set. Stand over there, point the camera, and I will direct myself.'

The crew remained silent as Kurtis walked back behind the camera.

'It's quite simple, Arlen. This is Dr Farquars room, it is his map. You are looking for a possible base where the Japanese and the Nazis might be meeting. Think about it. Why would Dr Farquar want to help you?'

Even though he was in character, Sal Klimer didn't want to be upstaged by Brandon Farlow.

'What about if this was a revolving table?' Klimer knew that the world always wants another action hero, whether he was fighting strange creatures, dinosaurs, ancient mummies, Nazis, or all of them put together, as long as it made money. He made a mental note to tell his agent to look for a film about Nazi dinosaurs in the desert. 'I'm thinking about a sequel here John. A sort of Indiana Jones, where I have sex with a lot of beautiful women, do you know what I mean?'

Klimer put in the vinegar stroke. 'Of course, it's your baby John. I mean, I wouldn't want to do an Arlen Parker sequel with any other director, unless this one doesn't go to plan…'

And so, we stopped filming whilst a rotating wooden disk was made, sprayed, and then displayed, on the dining room set. Just so Klimer could spin it around and read a map the right way up. It would also mean the camera would be focused on Klimer's face.

Brandon Farlow came back from lunch first (to be fair, he had not been back since breakfast). He saw the large wooden disk and slowly spun it around.

'Did I miss the buffet?'

'No,' said Kurtis. 'We thought it would be more interesting to show the map as a sort of globe.'

'But you could use this as a revolving buffet table?'

'Yes Mr Farlow. But it would mean just having to reshoot the scene one more time.'

'Perhaps with a bowl of peanuts, or a chip and dip?'

Some food was ordered. With that, we were ready to go.

Seventeen

We watched as Brandon came into the dining room, a hat fixed tightly on his head to cover the transmitter wire and earpiece. He went to where the map was now placed on a wooden wheel and fanned himself. Klimer stood on the other side of the table stroking his moustache. Myself (biting nails) and Kincaid (chewing cigar) went to one end of the table, so all of us could look at the map, and a camera could be placed on the fourth wall. Sitting somewhere behind the camera holding the script was Cameron, with a microphone plugged into a small radio transmitter. Kurtis called "action.".

Brandon, pointing at map: 'As you can see Mr Parker, none of the islands would be capable of having a meatball submarine dock near them.'

Klimer spun the wheel around so that he could read the map: 'What about Manila?'

Brandon, spinning the wheel back: 'Vanila ice cream The Nazis would have to cross international Roger waters, with the British Navy looking for Ladyboys. You must learn to love the Chinese way. Taxi 42, head down to Yangstzee Street and pick up one long dong.'

Klimer had no idea what Brandon was saying but stayed in character. As he spun the map around, Brandon spun it even faster. Behind the camera, Kurtis turned to Cameron.

'What the fuck has happened to Brandon's lines?' Cameron pressed a few buttons on the transmitter.

'I'm saying what's in the script, but the frequency keeps changing.'

Brandon, the old pro that he was, just repeated what was coming in his ears.

Brandon: 'Why are you this far south, Mr Arlen Parker pen. The Nazis are in Berlin, and the Japanese are over Cathay Pacific, travelling at thirty thousand feet, all clear to land. Car 54 looking for the cum of sum young guy.'

Behind the scenes, Kurtis turned back to Cameron.

'Change the frequency. Change the fucking frequency.' There was a whistle as Cameron tuned the little dials. Brandon spun the wheel as hard as he could just as Diddler came in. Klimer tried to stop the wheel and got a splinter.

'Use de plane, de plane,' said Diddler.

The camera kept rolling, even though no one had a fucking clue what was going on.

Klimer: 'I think the Nazis and the Japs are using this island as a base.' He pointed with his nose. 'And you are carrying out experiments without consent.'

Brandon: 'My work is more important than a shoplifting currently taking place at Woolworths. Any unit to assist. Perhaps if I show you what I do my House of Pain, you might see what I am trying to achieve.'

Klimer placed both hands down on the wheel, causing him to fall over. When he stood back up, half off his moustache was hanging off. Kurtis decided not to do a retake.

Cut to next scene.

    A courtyard filled with a large pond and various statues. In the darkness, Lara, dressed as Panther woman and Grayson walked past cages filled with various animals: gorillas, panthers, leopards (to be done by CGI later). Brandon appeared (with an orange). Klimer (holding his moustache) following. Grayson pulled Lara into the shadows. They watched as the two men went outside and towards the laboratory. Grayson limped after them.

Grayson (with limp and now with a very camp voice): 'Are you sure you want to be alone with him doctor Farquar. He might have a big one.'

Brandon: 'Don't worry, no man has yet been able to handle my Diddler.'

The midget followed as they headed down the dark passage as animals behind cages called out.

Kincaid and I, our sailors outfits now grubbier than before, walked across the courtyard to the fishpond. Lara jumped out of the shadows and threw feline glances at me.
Kincaid: 'Take us to Dr Farquar.'
Lara growled, then shimmied out of the courtyard. As we walked past the cages, I realised all the animals were staring at Lara.

The laboratory was straight out of the old Frankenstein movies. Large glass valves, ceramic resistors, and electric currents that would suddenly arc from one steel rod to another. Along one wall were rows of shelves containing glass bottles. Inside were what appeared to be body parts and various organs (the film crew had taken this literally, and inside one jar was a Xylophone). I went over to a bubbling vat of white liquid. Something inside slopped and wriggled, causing a white lump of goo to splash onto my face.

Brandon appeared from behind a row of tubes.
Brandon: 'My serum. After years of experimenting, I have created something which will one day be used to control the masses.'
We all look at the white serum.

Klimer: 'And you inject this into the Borlock's?'

Brandon: 'Or the arm, whatever's easier.'

On the table was a large bell jar. Inside was an unknown creature. A few pipes went into the liquid mixture, sending lights and tiny bubbles to the top.

Brandon: 'A mixture of Wokners and Borlocks.'

Me: 'Warlocks?'

Kincaid: 'Bonkers?'

Klimer: 'You think you are doing good, but all you have created is a monster.'

Brandon (pulling out an orange ball from his pocket): 'I will create millions of workers, hidden away, allowing the west to worry about shit they can't control, and feel good when they think they are fighting capitalism.'

Klimer (stroking his moustache): 'And what if the Borlocks don't agree with your utopia?'

As I chewed my nails, Kincaid chewed his cigar, and Klimer tried to chew the scenery, Brandon gave quite a good performance. He looked at the iron bars on a window.

Brnadon: 'That's why I have the Wokners to protect me. Communists like to think it can solve the world's problems, but it's always at the cost of someone else. As soon as they have money, they become the problem.'

Klimer: 'I'm not a communist.'

Brandon: 'No, you're an idealist. Brought up on feelings rather than facts, believing that your opinion is somehow the same as the truth. Unfortunately, it is not. Those in power will use every trick in the book to gain more power.' With this, Brandon peeled the orange he had in his hand, walked over to Diddler, and put the peel on the top of Diddler's head.

We turned as clapping and howling came from outside. Grayson limped in.

Grayson: 'Your Borlocks are turning blue.'

Brandon adjusted himself while eating the orange.

Brandon: 'If everyone could please get to the safety of the white house.'

We all left, leaving Brandon and Grayson alone.

Grayson: 'What shall we do with them, Dr Farquar?'

Brandon: 'They need distractions from distractions. Rather than Arlen Parker rooting around the island for monsters, let's give him something else to poke.'

Grayson: 'The panther woman? If she becomes pregnant, it will mean…'

Brandon smiled.

Grayson: 'What about his black friend?'

Brandon: 'Oh, I don't think she's quite ready for that yet. Best start off with a chipolata before you go chomping on a whole knockwurst.'

They walked outside.

Grayson: 'No, I mean what if he starts telling the Borlocks they are nothing more than pawns, they could demand real change.'

Brandon: 'My dear Monty. As long as the Borlocks are taking the serum, they are hardly going to topple over the statues.'

The men walked away. In the silence of an empty room, a faint light glowed on the operating table. The bell jar was now empty, the pipes left to drip onto the floor. A trail, and then tiny footsteps left a trail to the windowsill. Someone, or something, had escaped.

Eighteen

Another scene done. Brandon never did a second take. At least Klimer had learnt his lines. Now both decided to have a competition to see who could be the biggest dick on the island, slowing down every scene. The B Rolls, which were establishing shots, or anything that didn't include Brandon or Klimer, were being tagged onto the end of each working day. This often meant working well into the night. The only good thing was that sunset came at about five-ish and there were a lot of night scenes.

The real difficulty in the jungle is dealing with the bugs that are attracted to the spotlights. We had giant moths, insects with God knows how many legs, and the mosquitos, lots of fucking mosquitos. The idea of drinking gin because it was believed the botanicals helped keep the bugs away was quickly adapted to include vodka, rum, and pretty much every other spirit. The other big thing was smoking. People smoked as if they were trying to subdue a wasp's nest.

On set no one was allowed to smoke in front of the camera, unless it was in the script. The reason being continuity. If you had someone lighting up in the background, and you ended up doing ten takes, that could be ten fags some poor bastard had to get through. Behind the camera everything was a fire risk. Most of the things you see in a film are props soaked in chemicals; pretty much like the men that made them. So smoking was always done away from the set. This allowed people to partake in other substances apart from tobacco.

One night I was on my way back to the costume hut when I saw Cameron carrying a large shell.

'Is that a prop?'

Cameron shook his head.

'I found it the other day. Just makes you realise how beautiful and complex human nature is. The spirals are unique in that they start with the golden ratio, and because of their size, they move into the Fibonacci pattern.'

I didn't have a clue what he was talking about. 'It looks amazing. Have you turned it over?'

Cameron smiled. 'No, I've turned it into a bong.' He had put water and a thin metal tube inside the shell. He handed it to me and lit a small metal ball. 'Just purse your lips, and suck.' The draw was smooth and bubbly.

'Those spirals make all the difference.'

He had a go. He took in a full load, held it, then blew the smoke out.

'It's like God wants us to get high.'

'Lovely bubbly.'

As we stood in the jungle, I saw Klimer with Eve, the costume designer. I wondered if there was something more going on. The rascal, I thought. But my smile went as Lara came out of the hut. Klimer said something to Eve, then grabbed Lara, swooned her to the side, and kissed her. He then pulled her back up, then laughed and joked with Eve about the way Lara's panther costume moved. Moments later he repeated the whole thing again with Lara. The lousy piece of shit.

'Wow,' said Cameron. 'Being famous must be like putting your hand in a jar of tits. I bet he could do them both if he wanted to. I wish I had taken up acting.'

Right now, I felt as if I had vertigo, and it wasn't the spirals.

Nineteen

Fingertips have memories.
   Harvey Danger, Flagpole Sitta.

It was another nighttime shoot. Klimer was with Lara in the courtyard, teaching her how to speak. As they walked around the fishpond, I was filmed watching from the bushes (not in a pervy willy waver sort of way). As he was telling her about America, and how this crumby world could be heading towards war, she is distracted by my smell (again, not in a pervy smell my hand way, or even that fart made my eyes water way). Before Lara finds me, Klimer grabs her, and they kiss.

I waited and watched in the bushes. I knew I would never be as tall as Sal Klimer. He was well over 6ft. The ideal height for any film actor is about 5ft 10. Otherwise, the female lead has to stand on a box, or the camera constantly cutting to close ups of the actors faces. Klimer also had the chiselled jaw and muscular definition that comes from being able to afford to exercise every day, getting your teeth fixed, and only eating in the finest restaurants. I survived on pot, alcohol, and grilled cheese on toast. Later in life, I found out that women are smarter than what I thought. Be funny, that's the secret. But no man wants to be the sad clown.

When Kurtis said 'Cut,' and they stopped kissing, I could see that it meant nothing to Klimer, who checked his moustache in the pond. But Lara looked like a woman who had tasted a film star's tongue and liked it. I made a mental note to get fit, piss straight, and eat better…soon. It was then that I heard Klimer saying to the director 'can we just do that again?' Not because it needed doing again, but because the star wanted it done again. Klimer wanted Lara to crouch down a bit more, so he would appear slightly taller, and the camera behind her, so he could squeeze her tit.

They kissed, and kissed, and kissed. When it was over, Kurtis turned to me as I stood in the bushes.

'That's it. That's the look I want. The slightly retarded cabin boy who finally realises he will never get a woman like her because he just hasn't got it. Keep that face.'
The camera and the lights panned around to me so that I remained half in shadow. I could still see Lara and Klimer. I didn't even hear Kurtis say 'cut.' It wasn't until about an hour later that I realised I was alone on the set. I went back to the costume hut, picking up *Bridget Jones Diary* from the library (there were only two books, the other one was *Silence of the Lambs*, but I'm not really into farming).

Eve, the costume designer, was still up. I must have looked like a lost soul, and she quickly realised that it was the look of a man who had fallen in love with someone who barely knew they existed. Eve asked me if it was Lara. I didn't realise it was that obvious. All I had done since we got here was pine after her like a little puppy. I spent the next hour telling Eve about my problem, hoping she would give me an answer. She did. Eve told me that I was fantasising about an actress. The best thing I could do was to focus on my part (oo-err), no, my part in the script, do the best I could, and then see what happens after. A lot of people were counting on me to be professional. I agreed. I just didn't know what I was agreeing to.

#

When I saw Lara a few days later, she was on her way to make up. She wasn't happy. Her mum had sent a fax to Grayson's yacht. Some gossip magazines had reported that she and Sal Klimer were in a relationship. The problem was that Klimer was married to another actress, and America would paint Lara as the villain. She wondered who would spread such a rumour. My first thought was Brandon Farlow, or his little Diddler. And then I had a second thought (oh to be young again and be able to do it twice in one day).

Both of us were in our early twenties. We liked the same music, films, and life in general. I liked the fact that she was a bit posher than me, and I think she liked it that I was a likeable rogue, a talented chav, a working-class hero. I know there are parts in this book when you must be thinking "fuck off, you're a wanker," ok, but I was still likeable. "You're a bell end." Well not quite, more of a happy wanderer of life. "Cockwomble." OK, I'll give you that one. I'm just sort of being honest with how I remember things, and I suppose to many people I was a bit of a clown. Again, being honest, if that helped me get laid, then go fetch me a pair of oversized shoes and watch me juggle my balls.

'Why don't we start a rumour about us being in a relationship,' I said. 'You could get your agent to do a little piece on us in Maxim or Loaded magazine. You get a picture of you in a catsuit, I get my name mentioned, and everybody's happy.'

She said she would think about it. I told her that this was purely business. As long as no one got hurt, I couldn't see the problem. She said she would think about it. I found out later that what she was thinking about was whether she should have a public secret affair with me, or with Grayson Cunliffe.

'It's my big scene today,' I said, changing the subject. 'I've got to swim out to sea. Did you want to come down and watch?' That sounded so weak and pathetic that even I was embarrassed.

'No,' Lara replied. 'I'm helping Geno with his lines. Then I might go see Grayson and ask him for advice.'
I reluctantly agreed. Luckily, showbusiness is one of the few industries that doesn't thrive on gossip and innuendo.

Twenty

The scene was small, but important. I had to go down to the pier and swim out to the ship. One of the sailors who had an anchor tattoo on his forearm would refuse to let me on board. Another sailor with swallow tattoos on each hand would tell me he saw the sea glowing a milky white the other night, and they were leaving at the next full moon. I would then swim back and take a walk along the beach. I would find the broken lifeboat hidden in a cave. Finding a pair of binoculars, I look out to sea. A submarine begins to dive and disappears under a wave. I got it all done without a problem. The film crew were happy, and the director was happy that I looked so sad.

#

The next day news went through the island that another supply boat had arrived. As well as food, there were also crates of alcohol, lots of them. More prostitutes joined us. Their jobs were listed as: extra, physiotherapist, pipe technician, cheese maker, and manicurist. The Hollywood executives were busy with a journalist and photographer who had also arrived. The reporter was given a scripted account on how great things were between the two leading players. The photographer could take as many pictures as he liked, but they were going to be developed here.

I helped Cameron move a black oil drum into the jungle. Cameron twisted the lid off. It was filled with cannabis.

'Fucking hell. There must be fifty kilos of pure skunk in here.'

'Just under thirty,' Cameron replied. 'A present from Reg. If we don't go mad, it should last the film crew about a week.' The herbs began to open, letting off that pungent smell now found in most of the local parks in the summer.

Film crews are a funny breed. Some jobs are handed down from father to son, forming a Band of Brother's attitude between each unit. And if any actor is a bit of a cock, they are going to have a tough time on set. It also works the other way. One example is Daniel Craig. At the end of a film, he set up a small bar (which I think he learnt from Kincaid) and made the crew members cocktails. To have your martini made by James Bond is not something you are likely to forget. When rigging and lighting and prop units heard about his next film going into production, everybody wanted to work on it. When it came to Reginald Kincaid on a film set, he was a legend. Always said hello to everyone. Somebody's birthday, he was the first to buy them a drink. You needed a favour;

Kincaid would be there. Why am I telling you all this? Well, four large crates of Pot Noodle were waiting for me on the jetty.

Kincaid had a friend who worked in advertising. If we could get a picture of Brandon Farlow eating a Pot Noodle, it could be worth a lot of money.

'How will we do it?' I asked Kincaid as he drove a golf cart. 'Do we take a picture in secret?'
Kincaid held up his camera. 'We must have some integrity. Not much of course, we're actors after all. We will give him his Pot Noodles and simply ask for a private picture.'

We arrived at Brandon Farlow's trailer. Brandon sat in his chair, dressing gown open, an ice bucket on his head, water dripping down onto his large stomach and tiny balls. He picked up a tub of Pot Noodle.

'I knew you would come.'
Kincaid's camera accidently clicked.

#

That lunchtime Farlow had four Pot Noodles. He was obsessed with the bloody things. How can one person eat the same shit every day? It's not like McDonalds, where you have a balanced choice. Perhaps he knew it was upsetting Klimer, who always remained in character, and demanded everyone on set did the same. But you should never underestimate the ego of an idiot.

#

In my next scene I had to take Kincaid down to the beach. I see another creature in a rock pool.
Me: 'Captain Rimlick, look at this strange light green creature.'
Kincaid: 'What is it boy?'
I put my sword in the water.
Me: 'It feels like a type of octopus but has hairs on its face. And look, it has cleaned all the dirt off my sword.'
Kincaid: 'Sounds like what you've got there is a mild green hairy lips squid.'

When I went to show Kincaid the broken boat, it had gone. Brandon (wearing an ice bucket on his head), was being carried in his highchair. With him was Diddler, and a few Wokners.
Brandon: 'I could give you back your eyesight. But you will have to miss the next high tide.'
I stopped biting my fingernail and stepped forward.
Me: 'The other men won't like it captain, they were wanting to tug themselves off tonight.'

Kincaid: 'The poor bastards. We ran out of tissues three weeks ago. You promise we can leave once it is done?'
Brandon: 'You have my word as a former sailor myself.'
Kincaid: 'And you can make me see men again?'
Brandon: 'No, I'm just going to fix your eyesight. Is it a deal?'

"Cut."

There was still some dialogue left. We all turned.

Klimer arrived. He was not meant to be on set, so we knew something was up. Being an actor, he stood in front of the camera.

'John Kurtis. I have given my last acting performance for you.'

Kincaid whispered in my ear.

'I didn't even realise he had started?'

Klimer continued.

'You are without doubt the worst director I have ever worked with, and I know Oliver Stone.' Klimer turned and looked at the rest of the cast and crew. 'And this is the worst film crew I have ever witnessed. None of you know what you are doing. The story should all be about my character. I've been nominated twice, but you just don't know how to treat a real star. The public will only come to see this film because of me, not fat Farlow sitting on his fat arse.'

There was a bit of a gasp. If Farlow walked (in the metaphorical sense) the film would effectively be over. Brandon Farlow slowly scratched his face and turned to Diddler.

'Just remind me how many Oscars he has won?' Klimer turned back to the director. 'That's not important right now. Thanks to this contract I cannot leave the island. But you are going to get the worst acting since Jaws the Revenge.'

'Oh, come on,' cried Kincaid. 'At least pick a film that I'm not in.'

Klimer shouted at Kurtis. 'You need to change my character.'

'It's based on a bloody book,' Kurtis replied.

'Well, you've done plenty to help Farlow. He's wearing an ice bucket on his head. That isn't in the sodding book. Try doing something for someone who's career is actually going somewhere.'

'Stop,' called out Brandon. 'You've been complaining about being the better actor ever since we landed. Now let me give you a lesson in life.'

The film crew got a bit edgy. If Farlow tried to move a bit quick, that highchair could easily break, and Diddler would be squashed like a cheap burger bun. They watched as Brandon stood up. The highchair was set on a base, with two long poles, and then four legs, like an old-fashioned sedan. To get down on the ground he would have to traverse a series of steps.

'Careful,' said Klimer. 'I spent six months training as Owlman.' He stood in front of the highchair, held out his arms as if they were wings, and raised one leg.

Brandon turned as if to go down the steps backwards. He slowly bent over. And then he farted. When I say he farted, he didn't just blow a sharp G minor followed by a squeaky high octave. This was seven shades of deep filled Pot Noodles, a couple of hot dogs with mustard and onions, peanuts, and I caught the distinct smell of beans in tomato ketchup. It went on for a while. It opened with what sounded like a whale having a thrombosis and continued in the same vein for at least ten seconds, changing timbre slightly in the middle, but then a few seconds later it rose like a sexual trombone until it blasted out a glorious finale powerful enough to make a bear weep. What did it matter about winning two Oscars? Any man who can fart like that could wander the pubs of England for the rest of his life just performing that one trick. When it finally ended, we all waited in the breezeless heat as the smell lingered like paint made of hippo shit.

Klimer had taken the full blast. If he was going to say anything, the words had escaped him. As did his lunch. He turned to one side and threw up. When he had finished,

Brandon let out a smaller fart, ten seconds at most, but it was still heroic by any normal man's standards.

'Say cheese,' said the reporter, as the photographer next to him took a picture.

Klimer stormed off back to his trailer. Farlow turned to his audience.

'A good actor never misses his mark. A great actor knows exactly where he stands.' He took a bow, the crew behind him took a step back, and then gave a rapturous round of applause.

I knew exactly what I had to do to win Lara's heart.

Twenty-one

I waited to take my theatrical chance (is this a blagger I see before me?). John Kurtis and the Hollywood executives were desperately trying to fix the script. Klimer was not going to be the hero, and Brandon Farlow refused to re-shoot any of the previous scenes. Changing one of the main characters and the plot halfway through shooting was going to cause problems. Hollywood wanted a love story, even if Lara was half cat, half woman.

This was 1996. We'd had Mrs Doubtfire a few years before, and the idea of men and women not exactly being men and women. *Some like it Hot* was probably the best film to challenge sexual expectations. Being English, I had missed those American superhero comics (I used to get The Beano). Apparently, alien women with magnificent bodies were quite popular. *The Island of Dr Farquars Fiends* wanted to go beyond stereotypes and explore the idea of what they called non-binary sexuality. The executives were worried, even though the producers knew that panther woman would die at the end no matter what. It was in the book. With Klimer not bothering to get involved, someone still had to kiss the panther woman. The went for the financial choice first.

'Can we just do that again?' Grayson said as he held Lara. 'Perhaps if she came from behind and grabbed me as if I was a Tufted Tit-Mouse.'

So, it was done again, and again, and again. As I watched his lecherous hands crawl all over her body it was clear he was overacting on purpose. Lara repeated the scene, starting off hiding behind the trees, the statues, jumping in front of him, coming up behind him, cornering him; and all the time it felt as if I was the one being played. At least he kept his limp. I decided to go back to the costume hut to get changed.

'What's up love?' Eve asked me.

'Just watching Grayson with Lara.' I was going to say something about how difficult it is for a man to watch a woman he likes being kissed by someone else, when she spoke next.

'The love that dare not speak its name?'

I wondered what on earth she was on about, women's tennis? Someone else came in.

'Bit of a problem,' said Dexter, the assistant director. 'I need you to stand on Klimer's mark when Geno does his lines.'

'Where is Klimer?'

'Refusing to come out of his trailer before Farlow. I heard he's also smashed up the highchair.'

The crew had seen it all before. The on and off set shenanigans of stars and their whims. I went back into the jungle. Vietnam had a better production schedule than this film.

I waited as they set up the camera so that me and Geno would come out of the trees and see the huts where the Borlock's lived. Geno came up to me.

'Just give me the nod when you've finished speaking.' We walked until we found our spots in the dirt. 'Klimer being an arse wipe could be good for either one of us,' said Geno. 'It means more lines. Lara's been helping me go through some scenes. I think she's got talent.'

I was surprised, as she had never mentioned it. It would seem she was helping everyone but me. Ready. Village idiot scene. Take one.

#

Geno: 'We need to find out what's in that serum. These Borlocks seem less evolved than the Wokners. And the way they all obey Dr Farquar, it's like a prison camp with no walls. They are not fully animals, and not fully human.

They just wander around grunting inane slogans in the belief they are free.'

Me: 'Perhaps they're students?'

Geno: 'Let's see if we can get a closer look.'

We go through the jungle. At this point we are caught by the Borlock's. They take us to their camp.

#

The Borlocks crowded around us. Arlen Parker was meant to give a speech. I was going to say something, then Geno let out this mad, angry roar. The creatures stopped. It wasn't in the script. He did it again. The extras got the idea and moved back slightly. Then Geno took out his Zippo lighter. The flame causes some of the creatures to run away clapping, but not an old Orangutan mutant called Tango (no money for CGI, so this was all make up).

Geno: 'Your tribe is frightened. They are so used to being told what to think, they've forgotten who they really are. But I can help. I can give you freedom.'

The Borlocks, made up to look like a mixture of animals, mumbled between themselves. Tango gave a few claps, which seemed to calm the others down, then he turned to Geno.

Tango: 'Do you really believe the doctor will let you leave the island?'

Geno: 'You can speak?'

Tango lifted his neck to reveal a nasty scar across his throat: 'I used to be a Wokner; but when I started asking too many questions, they decided that something I did many years ago was now an offence.' Some of the other Borlocks also showed their scars. 'They silenced me and forced me into the village. Since then, I have been trying to help the others; teaching them to communicate through clapping. But if Dr Farquar was to find out, he would cancel us forever.'

Geno: 'It's better to spend a day as an orangutan, than spend the rest of your life trapped by the Borlocks.'

The sound of thunder came from the jungle.

Tango: 'The horn of Diabolos. Dr Farquar is coming.' The deep bellow was quickly followed by a high-pitched parp. 'And he brings his Diddler with him.'

As everyone runs out of the hut, Geno gives Tango his Zippo lighter. He now has the power of fire.

#

Dr Farquar and Diddler enter the village in a golf cart. How and why a golf cart had suddenly appeared in the middle of a jungle island in 1936, nobody seemed to know or care. Each scene was beginning to have more plot holes than a modern Disney film. Brandon and Diddler both wore silver ice buckets on their heads. Grayson rode behind them on a mini-Segway (just out of sight was Cameron on a bicycle carrying a radio transmitter), followed by a group of Wokner soldiers. Brandon pressed his earpiece.

Brandon: 'Kung Pow Chow Mein Fellini, cash only.'

He cracks his whip, and the Borlocks stand in line. We watch as Diddler and the Wokners take bottles of serum and inject the white fluid into the Borlocks. Brandon looks around. 'Where is the last of my big hairy Borlock's?'

Tango steps outside. Geno tells me to wait, and he steps outside as well. Everyone stops. Brandon adjusts the silver ice bucket on his head.

Brandon: 'You showed no fear. That's good breeding. I could use a man with your genetic characteristics.'

The line was meant to be said to Klimer when he was playing the character of Arlen Parker. When it was said in front of the character Lawton, the black assistant, even I noticed that the words now carried a different meaning from the script. Lawton, who as a black man in 1936 would certainly have known what it felt like to live in fear, ad libbed his reply.

Geno: 'Fuck you.'

The original character was meant to be played by someone else, the original reply was meant to convey stoicism, not anger. The camera kept rolling, and it was the best bit of the film so far. If they had made Geno Wright and Grayson Cunliffe the main characters, we would have had a hit on our hands. To his credit, Brandon stayed in character. Brandon: It was not a request, Mr Lawton; it was a scientific observation.'

#

As I walked out of the costume hut, John Kurtis was waiting for me.

'I'm trying out some new ideas,' he said. 'I want to re shoot the courtyard scene with you and Lara to see how things work.' He tapped his cowboy hat. 'I know your great grandfather is watching you.'

I replied that I wouldn't let him down. It meant a lot of script changes and learning more lines, but I was ready. Kincaid was pleased. He told me to keep the original Jack Bates character in mind; and show him making a mental and emotional journey as well as a physical one. Of course, all this went straight out of the window. I was already thinking of what colour my sports car would be. One of the executives also made a move.

'Hello,' he said. 'Artie Fufkin, Pollywood Productions.' Every so often his head twitched to the side. The man was a human Pez.

'Excuse me, where?'

'Pollywood Productions. Your English agent, Barry Hollocks, has asked me to represent you whilst you're on the island.' He gave a smiling twitch. 'I suggest we look at contracts when the film is complete. It gives us a bit more power when it comes to royalties.'

Power. I liked that word. Let's not kid ourselves; if anyone offers you anything, and in the deal are the words "power, and money," then the chances are you are going to be impressed. I was put off slightly by the way Artie Fufkin of Pollywood Productions would keep snapping his head as if he was being tasered, but at least now I felt like a star. My next scene was where captain Rimlick was about to regain his sight.

Twenty-two

Dame Helen and I sneaked into the laboratory. Brandon stood near the operating table, wearing a white cape, and the ice bucket on his head, which had a white towel wrapped around the top. He was still getting radio interference when they tried to feed him his lines, but he simply didn't care. Diddler was dressed the same. Grayson limped around wearing what looked like a nurse's outfit. Kincaid lay unconscious on the table, surrounded by surgical appliances, his eye patch removed, a light shining down on his face. Brandon beckoned us in.

Brandon: 'Lady Ruffsnatch, Master Bates, prepare to watch me become more powerful than God.'

Dame Helen (calls to her son): Montague, please come back with us. You could even bring that strange woman with you. If anyone asks about her bizarre accent and the way she licks herself, we could always say she's an exchange student from Grimsby.'

Grayson (shaking head): 'No mother. You are too old to understand that this is progress, this is the future. This must happen to save the planet.'

Dame Helen: 'Does that include wearing stockings? What if Mr Parker is right, and war is coming. You could be trapped on this island.'

Grayson: 'Don't you understand mother. Dr Farquar's ideas could mean the end of all wars. He is creating a society where everyone thinks the same, and nobody has to worry anymore because all our work will be done by his creations in the east of the island.' Grayson pulls down a set of large levers, electrical lights arc between two silver balls. 'Dr Farquar is the greatest genius in the world.'

Brandon takes out a Terry's chocolate orange and taps it on the top of Diddlers ice bucket helmet.

Theres then a bit where I try to take the straps off the (drunk) unconscious Kincaid. Dame Helen tells me to get the rest of the sailors as I am chased into the courtyard by some Wokner soldiers.

I run out and through the courtyard, where I am stopped by Lara. She is a bit more panther than woman (the serum isn't working). The script had been changed. Rather than run past her, we now kiss. This allowed my hands to rest on her arse as a tail falls out from the back of her dress. Being an actor of honesty and integrity, I did what all good men would have done.

'I'm sorry, could we just do that again?'

God may have the book, but the devil has all the best lines.

#

Monday morning came creeping like a nun. Literally. One of the hookers walked past the camp wearing a nun's outfit. My new agent, Artie Fufkin, Pollywood Productions, knocked on my tent with a cup of coffee for me. Most of it had spilled out due to his head twitching to the side like a soggy custard cream. He spoke about the Lord of the Rings audition. If this film goes well, it might not be for one of the Hobbits. Fairy tales and wizards are going to be big business, Artie said, because all the atheists are worried about the next millennium, and they are putting their faith in superhero's with human flaws.

I asked him about the hunt for a new James Bond. Too young. There was a war film in the works, due to be shot in England: *Saving Private Ryan*. Steven Spielberg was directing. Then Artie let out a big one. He apologised, twitched his head, and said the rumour of a new Star Wars film was true. It was like a dream. What the fuck Artie, you've got to get me on that. I could play a delinquent Darth, a sort of Catcher in the TIE. No, said Artie, that character is going to be a kid. But Obi Wan Kenobi to be played by a young actor, British, age range twenty-one to twenty-nine. Could I pull off a Guinness?

'Well, it's a bit early,' I replied, 'But fuck it, I'll have a pint with you.'

We walked over to the bar.

Of course, I should have stayed focused on the current project, learned my lines, followed the director's advice, been nice to everyone including the film crews, and dedicated myself into turning my dreams into reality. I didn't know it at the time, but as I sat there with a cold beer for breakfast, I was beginning to treat my life like one long holiday.

Later that morning I walked towards the beach. Theres something very manly about wading into the sea and having a really good piss. I found Sal Klimer churning up the sand in a golf buggy. His intention was to break them all so that Farlow had to walk everywhere. Lara came and stood next to me.

'What's he doing?'

'He's finally acting,' I replied. 'Acting like a giant arsehole.' Lara stood, arms folded, no make-up, wearing glasses (which I didn't know she did), and still looked great.

'Listen. I thought about what you said. About starting a rumour of us being in a relationship. I agree. It's a good idea. But this film is always going to come first, and I don't mean in the Biblical sense. I like you, but I'm here to work. Although, if things happen, they happen, agreed?' We did a pinky handshake. 'Did you hear they are casting a new Star Wars film.'

My first thought was that I hoped Grayson didn't find out. I then told her I might be up for the part of Kenobi.

She looked at me. 'The guy in Coronation Street?'

'No, that's Ken Barlow. Spielberg is doing a war film. I've been tipped to be in the cast for that.'

The life of an actor is not playing the part, its getting the right audition. You see, you might have to wait six months for a role to come up, and then the film might not go into production for another year. People who already had money, such as Grayson Cunliffe, could wait. For actors such as me, it was a constant struggle to either wait for a good character to come along, or work in a call centre to pay the bills.

Klimer continued to ride the golf cart up and down the beach. Brandon appeared in the other golf cart. He now wore a tin bucket with holes for eye sockets. Diddler had the same. Both carts churned up the sand as they raced past us.

'Do you think they are going to return to the jetty?' Lara asked.

I shook my head. 'Brandon has the high ground.

From the back of the cart Diddler picked up some Pizza Hut boxes and flung them at Klimer. One hit Klimer on the head, causing him to lose consciousness. The golf cart headed into the sea. The crew and the extras who had been watching suddenly ran towards him as Brandon and Diddler drove away. As some of the extras carried Klimer towards the medical hut and the crew pushed the cart back onto the beach I remembered that both carts used the same key. I took it out of the ignition.

'I'm off to see Brandon,' I said. 'Does anyone know if he is friends with George Lucas?'

Twenty-three

The only thing I can do is wipe my arse, brush my teeth, turn up, and do the best work I can.
   Tom Hardy.

The next few days were hectic. The script seemed to change every time I took a shit. I was wiping my arse with B Roll. With two camera crews working at full pace, everyone was on a set somewhere. I would go to sleep and dream about going to the Oscars. I was lucky. I would go on set and the director John Kurtis was clearly going insane. The heat, superstition and the Hollywood executives weren't doing him any favours. The next scene we did was not so much the end of the beginning, but the beginning of the end.

   I had decided that I would get my vitamin C intake by eating fruit for breakfast, leaving the coast clear for drugs and alcohol throughout the day. The hookers had decided to gang up on me, and not in the nice porno way. At every meal they would threaten me with a wet sausage, even when they weren't on the menu. I knew I was safe with the fruit, except for the bananas, and possibly the Kumquats.

I went down to the main set. Everyone was in the dining room. Kincaid, dressed Captain Rimlick, was wearing sunglasses. I kept thinking of Roy Orbison. We were all there, apart from Brandon Farlow and Sal Klimer. With only one working golf cart, they had decided that neither one would be the first to leave the trailer, and in so doing they kept waiting for the other to go up to the set. The shoot should have started at 9am. Two hours later, still no sign. At midday Kurtis made a decision.

'Reggie, you're close to Farlow. Go see if you can get him out of the trailer.'

'With what, a tin opener?'

'I should imagine the smell of bacon would do it. If we go one day over filming, we will have to book the island for another week; and they will break m y contract. Please.'

I went with him. Kincaid told me that another few weeks' shooting wouldn't just affect the director. Some of crew had other jobs lined up straight after this. It sounds terrible, but all I wanted to do was get famous. The less screen time Brandon and Klimer had, the more I might get.

Brandon was in his trailer, wearing a kaftan, his balls being gently fanned by Diddler. I wasn't even shocked by it anymore.

'How are you, old chap?' Kincaid asked.
Farlow looked over his belly.

'He's seen better days, Reginald.'

'It's just that everyone is waiting.'

Farlow was expecting this.

'What about Klimer?'

'He has a touch of mild diarrhoea,' Kincaid lied. 'Nothing serious. Said it will probably clear up by tomorrow.'

Brandon mulled the matter over, that is, over a leg of fried chicken. The thought of having Klimer struggle to do a scene as he desperately tried not to shit himself would be a delicious treat.

'Diddler. Fetch me my underpants and the ice bucket. We are going to make a movie.'

When he had dressed and we had driven him and Diddler to the set, I turned to Kincaid.

'What about Klimer?'

We drove to the canteen. After two of the hookers had kissed Kincaid and stroked their hands all over his body (what the hell does this guy get up to when I'm not around?), he told them he wanted some juice, to make "go poo poo." The hookers glanced at me as I sat eating a spicy chicken burrito. They handed Kincaid a bottle of green liquid. We then drove towards Klimer's trailer.

'What's in this?' I asked.

'Just something to relax him a little.' Kincaid replied. 'I think one of those girls has taken quite a shine to you, I bet she wouldn't even charge full price, you lucky devil.'

'Was it the one with the lazy eye and the facial hair who kept picking her nose and then dipping her finger into my lunch?'

Kincaid nodded. 'She reminds me of my mother.'

Klimer opened the door of his trailer.

'Why did Farlow agree to go first?'

'It was a meal scene,' I said.

Kincaid handed over the bottle.

'By the time you get there, all the food will have been eaten, and Kurtis doesn't want to stop until everything is done. You'd better have this energy drink. The natives swear by it.'

'No need.' Klimer went to the mini fridge and opened it. 'I've been drinking my own urine for the last few weeks, just like the old explorer's used to do.' He came back with a bottle of sand coloured liquid. 'You have the energy drink, I'll have this.'

I swallowed the green juice. It didn't taste too bad. Klimer finished before me. 'A bit tart. I should have got a bottle from the back. That one was still warm.'

He walked out of his trailer and drove towards the set, leaving the old captain and the young cabin boy to walk in the midday sun. I'm sure the green drink was nothing to worry about. When we got to the white house we were treated like heroes. In front of the crew, Lara came over, said I had saved the day, and kissed me. I had butterflies. You dream of kissing a beautiful woman, and when it happened to me I felt my face flush as some of the men on the set cheered.

Twenty-four

The scene was simple enough. After kidnapping the sailors on the ship and turning them into mutants, Brandon would discuss the merits of Captain Rimlick's eye surgery, believing that the end will always justify the means. It was now Geno Wright, as Lawton, the grandson of a slave, who would say that the idea was immoral. Absolute power would lead to the weakest in the world being exploited by the richest. Brandon, as Dr Farquar, would disagree, and use Lawton as an example of genetic conditioning. His ancestors were weeded out until only the strong were left. Sad to say, but this was in the original book. Dame Helen had raised concerns about the merits of slavery being spoken about in a modern film, but it was Geno who insisted that it stayed in. As far as he was concerned, hidden within the subtext about genetic experiments was the truth about racism; although I must be honest, I thought it said more about capitalism than anything else. As the camera moved into shot, a different type of shot began to rumble in my stomach as Klimer arrived.

Klimer stroked his moustache, Brandon (wearing ice bucket on head) ate a chilled Frog a la Peche, I chewed my nails, Dame Mivvy dabbed her face, while Kincaid (in sunglasses) drank half a pint of Cointreau and chewed his cigar. We were ready for action. And then Klimer took out a pair of the darkest sunglasses I have ever seen, gave them a clean, and put them on.

This ruined the scene, as it was meant to be about Captain Rimlick being temporarily blind. But Kurtis said nothing. As Klimer's began to talk, Brandon took out a penny whistle and began to play the tune to Hawaii-five-O, whilst Diddler stood on his chair and lifted the ice bucket hat, letting a pile of frozen prawns fell to the floor.

Watching such creative art take place, I realised I was going to shit myself, and John Kurtis finally lost it. He stopped filming and told Brandon and Klimer that they were not only wasting their time, but more importantly, the time of every other person on set. As he went on, I could feel my gut churning. I ran out and took a dump in the jungle. By the time I turned around to wipe my arse on a leaf, I realised I had shat in the golf cart. It was a nasty one. The Hitler of all shits. It was still bubbling as I walked back onto the set. Klimer was trying to pass the buck.

'It was Reginald. He wasn't ready.'
Kincaid stood up.

'How dare you. How fucking dare you. I've never missed a cue in my life.'

'Certainly not the queue to the bar.' Klimer replied.

I wasn't going to let Klimer take the piss out of my mate.

'Don't talk to him like that.'

Klimer looked at me as if he had only just realised I was in the scene.

'Who the fuck are you?'

Dame Helen's stood up. 'His name is Leslie Smells, and he is being more professional and more of a gentleman than you.'

Klimer disagreed. 'I've been nominated two times.'

'Harvey Weinstein may have paid for the tuxedo,' Helen replied. 'But I'm afraid you have neither the wit nor the humility to understand that to be a good film actor you must be aware that every other poor sod on this island is also part of the process. And I have actually won an Oscar, and a BAFTA, and a Tony, and an Olivier; and after forty years in the business, let me give you some advice. Stop acting like a pair of cunts so we can finish this bloody film, and all go home.'

She walked off stage left to a round of applause from the crew.

Klimer got into the golf cart and then jumped out. A monkey in the tree laughed as Klimer walked back to his tent. Brandon Farlow smiled and stayed for the reshoot. In truth, he knew he had lost the ability to act well when he reached seventy. Years of good living had ruined his appetite to put any effort into his craft. He also knew the director was too weak to tell him what to do. He calculated the effort it would take to be professional in front of Dame Helen Mivvy, and felt the cost would be worth it. Besides, he was enjoying the young prince Klimer lose his sanity. This film had reached the halfway point, and the two main stars had already given up.

I found Kurtis in the jungle smoking yet another cigarette.

'Give me Klimer's role,' I said. 'Let Geno save the creatures, and I have the loves scenes with Lara. You probably wouldn't even have to change much of the script.' He nodded (although he was on so much medication it may have just been a nervous twitch). I finished the scene knowing that the Best Supporting Actor category in my dreams was quickly being replaced with just Best Actor. In more ways than one, I was feeling quite flushed with myself.

#

In the laboratory, Brandon confirmed with Grayson that the operations on the sailors had gone well, and that panther woman was in heat. Someone needed to have sex with her in the next few days.
Grayson: 'You may have noticed I have a slight limp, Dr Farquar. It is an old rowing boat injury.'
Brandon: 'Caught in the rollocks?'

Grayson: 'No, just the upper thigh.' He went to a cage and looked at the creatures that had once been sailors, now apes and beasts. 'When will we send out the first batch of workers?'

Brandon: 'Soon. Think of it Monty; a world where people are picked because of their genetic characteristics rather than talent. I just need to make sure the serum keeps them under control.'

As they walked out of the laboratory they did not notice that up in one of the high windows, Tango was watching.

Twenty-five

Doing re shoots for me meant the whole crew had to come back. If the other sets were busy, we would change location or shoot at night. I began to lose track of where we were in the story, as I was doing scenes that had been done weeks before. I also realised how difficult it was to be the lead actor. The directors would do the scene, then ask me to do it slightly differently, and do it again, and again, and again.

    Pre-dinner cocktails had become a regular thing if we were not on a night scene. Reginald was the bon viveur behind the bar. He could sell a pair of sunglasses to Van Gogh. Dame Mivvy knew pretty much everyone who had been in the business since 1956. Being one of the youngest on the island, I had that naïve (gormless) likable look that made older actors want to talk to me. I enjoyed listening to their stories. My only problem was that being so young in showbusiness, I couldn't drink as much as the others. On a rare night off, Cameron's conch and Kincaid's cocktails soon had me hammered. Maybe it was the glorious surroundings, the exceptional company, or perhaps the idea that the whole universe had somehow looked down and given me a chance to be someone; but I was feeling horny.

And then Lara and Grayson came up to the bar, followed by a man holding a camera. I was going to say that I couldn't say what I disliked about Grayson; but I knew what it was. In American films anybody can be rich and powerful. You watch a guy in his twenties driving down the freeway, you don't know if he is a businessman, a celebrity, comes from family money, or is a broke cowboy. When I watch an English film, I question the social framework in every shot. Terraced houses, it's the north. Big house in the country, it's a Tory. As soon as the actor spoke, I would know exactly what sort of family they had been brought up in, what their education was like, and where they were likely to end up. Grayson Cunlick would never know what it would be like to have to serve someone else; to have to behave in a certain way just to get paid, to worry if you would have enough money to fix your car.

Grayson called out to the bar.

'Drinks for everyone. I've just been told I'm up for a BAFTA.' He picked up the BAFTA on the bar. 'I could use this to work on my speech.'
Dame Helen wasn't so sure.

'Isn't that a little bit premature? No pun intended Reggie.' Grayson studied the BAFTA. It was a bronze mask. 'Lara wants to know how it would feel to be at the awards. I admire anyone with ambition who wants to do something with their life, rather than just play acting. You know Dame Helen; Lara very much reminds me of you.'

'How?'

Grayson held up the mask. 'Well, you know, a girl from a nice upper middle-class family who knew acting was her passion.'

'Upper middle class?' Helen replied. 'First of all, I grew up in a two up two down terraced house in Manchester. I'd never tasted a Jaffa cake until I was twelve. And as for acting, believe me, times were very different when I started. Every production company had a casting couch; and they were tough in those days. I didn't realise "DP" stood for "Director of Photography" until I was on my fifth film. The only reason I got into acting was to get out of the shit-hole I were trapped in. No offence Leroy.'

'None taken,' I replied, impressed by her determination to give me a different name every time, and that she had a slight northern twang when she was angry.

If Grayson had said nothing more, I probably would have left it. If he had gone up, collected the award, thanked his agent, and gone back to his yacht, I would have taken it. But he never. Like all actors when asked to improvise, he couldn't help himself from walking and talking at the same time.

'To be, or not to be. That is the question.' He glanced at me. 'That's Shakespeare.'

I wanted to tell him how much I hated his type; people who could afford not to work for months on end to save themselves for parts; whilst better actors had to live in the normal world. I wanted to tell him how I thought his political views, demanding equality for all while living in a big house, having accountants explaining how to avoid paying taxes, and no doubt sending his own children to a private school, was just bullshit. I wanted to tell him that life hits the poor harder than he could ever imagine. I had so many things I wanted to say.

'Wanker.'

Grayson stopped.

'I beg your pardon?'

'You heard me.' So much for my big speech. 'Fuck the BAFTA's. You're just living their lies.' (Now I was turning into Oasis).

Grayson could see I was drunk and angry. Even if he could beat me in a fight, he didn't want to get an injury. 'Look old chap. It's 1996, not 1936. No one is impressed by how much an actor can drink. Why don't you focus on the film?'

That was too much.

'Why don't you suck my balls.'

Grayson grew a bit of courage.

'Well, Shakespeare must be kicking himself that he didn't come up with that soliloquy.' He then made the fatal mistake.

'You know, I don't think you should stay in the film business. You're not in the same league as myself and Lara.' He smiled, convinced he had won.

I took a shot of tequila.

'Right, you fucker.' And I went after him.

He ran around the campfire.

'I must warn you; I have a heart condition.' He was a slippery sod. Like trying to catch the clap from a nun. 'Look, it's not what you think. There is really nothing going on. It's all an act for the reporters.'

We kept running around in circles until he tripped, landing over a wooden table. I picked up the BAFTA award and held aloft the small gold mask.

'In the words of Hamlet, I am going to shove this right up your arse-hole.' I grabbed hold of his cargo shorts and pulled them down.

'Liam, stop.' Dame Helen had finally remembered my name. She held up her Oscar. 'Use this. It will be more cinematic.'

As I went to collect my award, Grayson pulled his shorts up and ran down towards the beach.

'Well,' said Kincaid. 'If award shows were more like that, viewing figures would go through the roof.'

'I don't mind actors showing off,' said Dame Helen. 'That's part of the performance. But when they start to be bully others, that really gets up my arse. No offence Liston.'

I took a bow.

'Liam.' It was Lara. She didn't look happy. 'What the hell do you think you're playing at?'

I held an award in one hand.

'It was his fault,' I said. 'He said that I seemed to have gone into showbusiness by mistake.'

'Do you think this is funny?' She clearly wasn't happy. 'This is my career, not some holiday in the sun where you go around getting pissed every night.'

'You can do better than Grayson Cunlick,' I said. If I had left it there, I might have got away with it; but I had to continue. 'And Sal Klimer.'

Lara shook her head. 'You're worse than both of them. Do you know why? Because you think everything is a joke. No one takes you seriously because you don't take yourself seriously. They may act like a pair of arseholes; but at least they are willing to put the work into being one. You still think it's funny to do everything half-arsed.' She put the award down. 'Nothing will ever happen between Grayson and me, for the obvious reason; and nothing happened with me and Sal Klimer. But even if it did, what on earth has it got to do with you?'

I thought it was over. I was wrong. She has an encore.

'I'm tired of always having to worry about what I do because some jealous boyfriend is stupid enough to believe that what they see on a screen is real. Be yourself Liam. You'd probably be a nice person if you weren't so desperate for fame.'

She walked off towards her tent.

Kincaid poured me one for the sand.

'Award shows are overrated,' he said. 'Bow tied hives of scum and villainy. The best performances on the night are from the waiters who try and pass you their script. Avoid them and producers like the plague dear boy.'

I put a bread stick into a jar of dip and took a bite.

'At least the food here is good,' I said. 'What is this, cheese and chive?' I put another dollop into my mouth.

Dame Helen picked up the jar.

'No. It's my haemorrhoid cream. Try not to eat all of it; I've got to ride in the bloody golf buggy with Brandon Farlow tomorrow.'

I finished my drink. Reginald Kincaid helped me to my canvas slumber, and that night I hoped that nothing else would go wrong.

Twenty-six

If only you'd tell us, we'd let you go.
    Supergrass, Caught by the Fuzz.

Back in England, Chief Inspector Bastad had shouted at other officers to find out who had taken the registration plates. Not surprisingly, he didn't seem to be getting very far. The best line of enquiry he had was in the photography department. Murder cases were stopped whilst people worked on enlarging the car. A silver Ford Escort, late 1988 model, possibly over a thousand in the country that age and colour. Bastad didn't care. He had daily briefings. He got intelligence to find out how many cars were registered within ten miles of where he had sat in the van. The driver and passenger remained blurred, but there was something on the dashboard. The forensic scientist moved the magnifying glass away.

    'Ah yes, they appear to be Vincent and Jules.'
Bastad grabbed the magnifying glass.
    'You know the offenders?'
    'No,' the forensic scientist replied. 'The bobble dolls on the dashboard. From Pulp Fiction. The film.'
Bastad had no idea.

'There's a film called "From Pulp Fiction?"'

For the next few weeks specialist units were driving around looking for a silver Ford Escort with two dolls on the dashboard.

My mate Billy Custard was a creature of habit. The Studio café, his drug dealers flat, the job centre, The Red Lion pub, The Golden Plaice chip shop, and regular cruises up and down the high street to stare at women. We liked guitar music. Oasis were good, but the Stone Roses were the band that hit us as we became teenagers. We knew every song on the first album. It was the soundtrack to our lives. They were the reason I would never wear a tie.

After breakfast in the Studio Cafe, Custard was on his way back that afternoon to his mums. The music was up, I am the Resurrection, and the windows were down. Custard saw the blue lights and had the mint in his mouth before the copper had even got out. He didn't know that the police officer was technically committing an offence for driving a marked car whilst not on duty. This one was even smiling as he got closer and bent down to stare into the window.

'Left the sausages in the frying pan, sonny?'

Custard turned down the Stone Roses album in the CD player.

'I was just on my way to my nan's house officer, to make sure she gets her medication.'

Bastad saw the bobbleheads on the dashboard and kept smiling.

'What's her name?'

'Sally. Sally Cinnamon.'

'And who's your mother, Yoko Ono?' Bastad took out his baton. 'You are going to make my job a whole lot easier if you tell me where the pot is.' He took a deep sniff. 'Let me guess; Acapulco Gold, laughing gravy, the old Sgt. Pepper's boot polish. You worthless fucking hippy.'

'Dude, take it easy.' Billy Custard may have been more working class than chips, but he was not a fighter. Most of the time he could charm his way out of things. This copper seemed to be wound tighter than the others. Bastad opened the door and shouted.

'Get out of the car.' He took Billy's mobile phone. 'Not a bad score on snake.' With that he dropped the phone onto the ground. 'Whoops a daisy.'

Bastad then pulled out the portable CD player. 'I'm in the wrong job. It must be great being a drug dealer, driving around all day, listening to hippie music, being able to shit money, dodging speeding tickets.'

The last bit jolted Custard Billy. Is that what this was all about?

Bastad looked as if he was about to drop the portable CD player.

'Do you understand what I'm saying?' He waited. 'English. Do you speak English, you little fart knocker? You know what a speeding ticket is, don't you? You know certain drugs are illegal, don't you?' He pushed Bill back onto the path, then went inside the car. In his left pocket was a bag of green weed. Put that in the car, and it was a police caution. In Bastad's other pocket was a bag of red and yellow ecstasy pills.

'When I find them, you will spend a few months in prison, sucking on some old lags everlasting gobstoppers. Unless you want to tell me about the speeding tickets?'

Bastad also wanted to get young Bill to confess to taking the old police van registration plates, and he wanted the real name of that other little shit who had been involved. He wanted to see both in court, taking the points and the fines. He wanted those little figures on the dashboard. As he was to later write in his statement: I reached into the car and pulled two men off.

'Vincent and Jules.' Bastad broke the plastic bottom of the Jules figurine. He then slipped the bag of drugs into his palm. 'Well, well, well,' he said with a smile. 'You've remembered the policeman's motto. If in doubt, it's always the black guy. I have you now, young Willy Custard.'

Chief Inspector Bastad turned off the tape machine.

'Do you read the Bible, Mr Custard? The path of the righteous man is beset on all sides by the inequities of the selfish and the tyranny of evil men. Blessed is he who, in the name of charity and good will, shepherds the weak through the valley of the darkness, for he is truly his brother's keeper and the finder of lost children. What about our two little friends Jules and Verne? Let's call them exhibits one and two. Filled with twenty-four ecstasy tablets. What if I was to say to you, I could make those pills disappear, just like my finger in your mum's hairy hammock. All you need to do is confess to the speeding tickets.'

Sat in the police interview room, Billy Custard thought about it.

'I didn't know about the drugs; and as for speeding tickets, I haven't got a Scooby Doo what you're talking about.'

Bastad showed Billy blurred images

'Confess to the speeding tickets,' said Bastad. 'It could save you, and your friend.'

Billy thought about it again. 'If I do admit the speeding tickets, the drugs will go away?'

Bastad nodded. 'Just give me your friends name.'

'Jack Bates,' said Billy continued. 'But you wont be able to speak to him. He's gone on holiday by mistake.'

Twenty-seven

As well as getting more time in front of the camera, I found I liked writing the script as well. Kurtis let me because he believed his spirit guide was happy that I was just updating my own family history. In truth, I could see he was losing the plot. He was up all-night chanting and then zonked out during the day while executives all gave him more demands.

Weeks in the jungle was also having a strange effect on the cast and crew. The extras stayed in costume to take drugs and have sex. The results were a cross between a Spielberg movie and a porn film. So much so, that everyone started to call their camp site "Jurassic Poke." Most of the technical crew were still in the same clothes they had arrived in. No point wasting valuable drinking time by having a shower. The hookers were enjoying themselves cooking and dancing. The executives were happy we had enough in the can to release something. That's the crazy secret. The producers know when a film is bad, and they are still winning to release it because they own the advertising companies, the tv talk shows, and the cinemas. When a film makes a loss, the money is picked up somewhere else. The real secret is that the film companies also own the actors. If you're in a film that makes a loss, your price goes down, and you take jobs you wouldn't normally take.

Grayson gave me a public apology. Lara had come to him and asked to have a few pictures to get the gossip columns going back home; but there was nothing between them. I apologised as well, although I couldn't help noticing Grayson would stare at men when he thought I wasn't looking. At least he wasn't staring at Lara.

One night we were sitting on the beach, going through the lines that I had written, drinking our cocktails. She had an idea about my character teaching her character how to speak again. I said I would tell Kurtis a group of witches had come up with the idea, and he would probably buy it. I then thought, maybe I should direct it? When Lara sked me how I would picture the scene, I gave her a practical run through.

We kissed. Our hands moved over each other. She looked to make sure the beach was deserted.

'Do you have any protection?'
I nodded. 'I got holiday insurance through Equity.'
We began to take out clothes off. I like tits. I like looking at tits, I like squeezing tits, and I like sucking tits. Lara didn't want to take her top off. This was pretty much going to be a missionary encounter. Now I had the difficulty of either keeping my shorts half on and worrying about the zipper scratching my sandy balls. Or taking them off completely and

worrying about the bugs biting my arse. We adjusted ourselves (Lara and me, not my balls). Now I had another thing to worry about. Keeping it hard didn't seem to be a problem. Keeping it going for as long as possible was the issue.

I have my ways of slowing down. Think of any Kevin Costner film. Remember my seven times table. What's the recipe for spaghetti bolognaise? I needn't have worried. For anyone reading this book, I was bloody brilliant at sex; longer than the director's cut of The Lord of the Rings (no, she wouldn't let me, you rascal).

Doing it outside is a strange experience. You have to keep looking around to make sure you don't get caught, which slows you down. But it also adds to the excitement, which speeds things up. To which, with the encouragement of Lara, I certainly did at the end. I thought my spine was going to snap. Once the music stopped playing and the fireworks were over, I gently held the woman of my dreams in my arms and sweetly whispered those beautiful loving words into her ear.

'How was it for you?' (To be honest reader, I didn't care). She kissed me. 'Let's take a dip.' And now she took her dress off.

We walked into the sea. The cold water quickly shrivelled my manhood. I was also worried about swimming naked.

Nobody wants some fish having a nibble on their nob in the dark. Lara came close to me.

'Please speak to Kurtis about me having more lines in the script.'

I had already written them and directed the scenes in my head. I agreed. I was staring at her nipples at the time, hoping she would get closer. She went back to the beach. I should have realised at the time what was happening. I think that's what they call Post Nut Clarity.

She put her clothes on without any problems. I ended up just getting sand on my balls and in my arse crack. We walked back to the camp, hand in hand. But she let go when we saw the lights. Lara went towards her tent. I went to get a drink. Kincaid was sitting on a bar stool reading a book.

'I hope you didn't catch crabs,' he said.

'I haven't been with the hookers.' I zipped up my shorts. He explained that it was crab season, and the creatures would be heading towards the shore. How they knew it was mating season was just one of the wonders of the universe. He then asked how shagging Lara went?

Pretty bloody good, actually.

#

The next morning a couple of Hollywood executives gathered around John Kurtis to give him the bad news. They were firing him and getting in another director. Kurtis pleaded with the executives to let him stay. This film had been his baby, he had been working on it for the last six years. He had slaved over every scene, worried about every word, imagined every frame time and time again. He had done everything in the natural and supernatural world to get this film made. Without him, no one would be here. But he had forgotten the golden rule in Hollywood: Money talks, bullshit walks. Klimer was staying, Kurtis was going. Under his contract, he was not allowed to speak about the film until after it had been released. There was a boat waiting for him at the jetty.

Twenty-eight

We've gone on holiday by mistake.
    Withnail and I.

News quickly went around the island. Luckily, showbusiness isn't riddled with innuendo and gossip, nor is it filled with narcissists only worried about themselves, and especially not drama queens who love the big productions.
The sound of a gunshot made me jump. I ran down to the Hollywood executive's camp.

Kurtis was standing next to a silver trailer, demanding Klimer to come out. His exact words were.

'Klimer, you clunt. Come out and face me like a man.' He drank from a half empty bottle of Jack Daniels. 'Come on out ya pish drinkin bastard.'

A few people tried to calm him down, but Kurtis was having none of it. He climbed onto the roof of Klimer's trailer, lifted an air hatch, and pissed down into it. Kurtis kept shouting as he jumped down and banged on the door. It was only the sound from another helicopter that caused Kurtis to stop and run into the jungle. By the time Klimer come out, Brandon Farlow was on his third Pot Noodle.

#

Jane Dough had previously directed a film based on the life story of Sigmund Freud's wife, Martha Bernays, called *I wish he had a bigger one*. It had been nominated for an Oscar but didn't win. The publicity it created allowed the media to question why no female had ever won Best Director. What was needed was a film that had all the right ingredients to be in with a chance of winning, and a woman to direct it. The executives hoped *The Island of Dr Farquars Fiends* was the one.

With her worn out baseball cap, khaki T shirt and ripped shorts, she looked like a Lara Croft lesbian wet dream. She had met with the crew first and told them she wanted to be out of here on schedule, and on budget. She had been offered a three-picture deal to finish this crap, and those that helped were more likely to work with her again. She won their hearts by saying she didn't care what happened offset, but they were going to leave the island with a film in the can. Ironically, behind her another large can of cannabis was wheeled up into the jungle.

Then she came up to the actor's camp.

'I've seen the script,' said Jane. 'And it's no Schindler's List. It's not even Mengele's Memo. But I am going to finish it…with some changes.' Jane Dough was not a director who was waiting for the cast to ask questions. She was merely pausing for breath. 'Sal Klimer is not the headline act anymore. I've got enough clowns in my circus to make him go juggle his balls somewhere else; and that counts for all of you.' She walked slowly along the line, similar to those war films where the leader lines up the team. 'I still want this film to be a nomination contender. I will meet each of you in turn in the editing hut to discuss what changes to the script I am going to make.'

When it was my turn, I explained that I had been helping to write the scripts, as I was related to the author. Her reply was short and sweet. 'So what?' she wanted the film to be an ensemble piece. The theme would be on how power corrupts, and that justice was universal rather than man made. The ending would be kept the same. The problem was the film still needed a love interest just to get women into the cinema to watch it. I handed her the scenes I had written so far. Most of them were of me kissing Lara even though she was in a catsuit.

The female director summed up the situation.

'Well, somebody's got to stroke that pussy and make the audience think she's pregnant.'

I was pleased.

Jane continued. 'It might as well be you as the gormless cabin boy who falls in love.'

I was delighted, but felt I had to defend myself.

'That's brilliant, but I wouldn't say gormless.'
She waved me away.

'He's this retarded goofball who's almost an experiment himself; a half-wit moron who nearly destroys everyone on the island because he happens to be attracted to someone out of his league.'

'Well, I wouldn't say I'm half witted.'

'A strange idiot who's never had sex before and ends up with a farmyard animal.'

'Have you been talking to the hookers?'

Jane stopped me. 'Yes, it might work. I could keep the Arlen Parker character in for the Nazi element. Nazis are always good box office. I wouldn't have to change that many scenes. I suppose I could keep Grayson and Geno in the loop as well.' She looked at me. 'Can you do it?'

I nodded.

'I know all the lines.'

Jane stopped.

'Lines. Who gives a fuck about lines? This is Hollywood. You just need to know how to fire a gun and kiss the girl.'

At this point Kincaid knocked and came in.

'Am I too early for my close up?'

Jane Dough looked at the old actor.

'Do you know what the Warner brothers said was the most dangerous creature known to man?'

'A lesbian Nazi?' Offered Kincaid.

Jane shook her head. 'An actor who thinks they know more than the director. If I catch either of you doing it, I will shoot you with a real gun. Do I make myself clear?'

Kincaid nodded. 'Of course. By the way, have you ever had the pleasure of working with Brandon Farlow and Sal Klimer before?'

Twenty-nine

More scenes were quickly re-shot for the third time. There wasn't that much, it was mostly me matching up my eye line with previous shots of panther woman so that we were the ones who appeared to be looking at each other. Brandon Farlow refused to re do the scene where they talk about Arlen Parker; instead, the name Jack Bates was simply dubbed over. We soon began to catch up with the filming schedule. The crew were old pros; as long as they turned up and worked during shooting, Jane didn't grief them if they started drinking as soon as they were finished. Even the hookers were happy. That might have been due to the box of super-lube ribbed condoms that had come in on the last boat.

As for Sal Klimer, his character of Arlen Parker would still be the hero, but more of his lines were given over to Geno Wright. The executives umm'd and ahh'd over having a film where a black character was seemingly more important that a white character. At the time, The Shawshank Redemption hadn't made much money at the box office. The issue was resolved by giving Klimer a glorious death. The only difficulty was going to be the upcoming scenes where Arlen Parker had to be on set with Dr Farquar. My time on screen had been doubled, I had a couple of big speeches, and I had got Lara a few lines. This was possibly the greatest time in my professional life. The idea that I could win an Oscar seemed to be in my hands.

Later that day Lara came up to me in my tent.

'Jane has spoken about giving me a bigger slot. Thank you. How was filming today?'

I told her I hadn't thought about it. I was now dreaming of acceptance speeches, fast cars, big houses, and people just in awe of me simply because I was me. I promised I would see Lara later. But honestly, I was only in it for the sex. She was always wanting to talk about the film production, when I was already at the premiere.

Thirty

Panther woman now had a name: Lola. L, O, L, A, Lola. Another evening scene at the white house. Inside, the guests were listening to a speech on the radio about Stalin's new Great Purge and the Berlin Olympics. Sal Klimer, who as Arlen Parker, had watched his lines cut down next to nothing, still wanted to play up. He stroked his moustache with his middle finger, and then suddenly stopped the scene.

'Jane. You need to move the backlight.'

'No, I don't,' Jane replied. 'Go back to the last line and keep rolling.'

Klimer held up his hand.

'I think the light should be dimmed, and the camera positioned for an over the shoulder shot at my face.'

Jane came from behind the camera and rested a hand on Klimer's shoulder.

'Sal, if you ever try and direct me again, I'm going to shove that boom microphone so far up your rusty sherifs badge, you could brush your teeth with it.'

Klimer finally did what he was told.

#

The next scene was me and Lola in the courtyard. I told her about what life was like in London. The underground trains, airplanes that were like ships but flew in the sky; and something new called television, which promised to show you Jesse Owens in the 1940 Tokyo Olympics while you are sitting at home. I unwrapped a flag to reveal the Charlie Chaplin figurine I had taken from the ship. I explained that he was the most famous clown in the world. He was an actor in Hollywood, someone pretending to be something they are not. I handed it to her as a gift.
Lara: 'What is a clown?'
Me: 'Someone who makes others happy, even though he might be sad.'
Lara: 'What is happy?'
Me: 'When you can't stop thinking about someone and smiling all the time. It's a bit like being in love.' I was ready to go in for the kiss.
The cat woman purred as she rubbed the ships flag on my face.
Lara: 'Do you like touching cloth.'

I put the Charlie Chaplin figurine at the base of one of the statues. As I did so, Lola looked down at the pond. As she stared, her eyes became the same as a cat, and her claws extended out of her fingers. When I came over and put a flower in her hair, she jumped up kissed me. Behind my back she looked at her hand. The claws would not retract. A tear ran down towards her furry lips.

Thirty-one

Jane was asking for more help writing out the new scenes. In truth I was losing motivation. I wanted to be the hero, not the bloody servant. I didn't have the discipline to stay focused on the present. My future was all about getting that Star Wars audition. The past was yours, but the futures mine, as the Stone Roses once said. Yes, get off the island, wait until the film was released (the date was going to be around Christmas/New year, the best time for the members of the academy to see it), then hit the promotional circuit with the rumour that I was going to be in the biggest franchise in the galaxy. It felt like that moment when Luke looks at the two-moon sunset and knows he must leave. I sat on the beach and lit a light sabred size joint.

Here on the island the sun went down quicker than Monika Lewinsky being offered an internship. Within in the space of one cocktail you went from wearing sunglasses to needing a torch. Now, of all the people I expected to come up and talk to me in the dark, Grayson was probably the last. We had been on talking terms on set, but outside of acting there wasn't much else. I was hoping he would just say "Hello," and walk on. Instead, he sat down, so close to me that our legs were touching. He looked out at the last of the sunset.

'I'm hoping you can feel it to?'

I wondered if he was talking about the spliff. Perhaps he had a message from Lara. Whenever I thought about that body, my nob went as stiff as an old motorbike kick starter. Grayson continued.

'I suppose you've realised that…you know.'

I didn't have a clue about…you know, so I wasn't really sure where this was going. I looked at the orange embers on the end of my large one. It was then that something really weird happened. Grayson put his hand on my leg.

Now, I've got friends I've known since school who were as camp as a row of tents, and it never bothered any of us. I've also made new friends, especially within the acting world. Again, being gay didn't matter. Straight people were offered gay roles, and gay men were offered straight roles. Some of the straight people I've worked with were very tactile. But this felt…different.

'I'm glad you got the role,' said Grayson. 'But obviously the only reason I needed Lara was as a beard for my role.'

What the fuck was he was talking about…a sausage roll? And who had a beard?

And then Grayson's hand moved up to my knee.

'I think I know how you knew.'

'I only know now what you knew then,' I replied.

'And you knew because I know what you're going through.'

Was this a Noel Coward play? I took a long drag... ... ...

'What is it that you actually know?'

Grayson's hand was still on my knee.

'I know that whatever games consenting adults want to do in private is fine. Do you agree?'

I hoped my next question was the right one. 'Don't tell me you've got a PlayStation on the boat?'

For some reason this seemed to surprise Grayson. He wondered if I was playing mind games.

'Let me get this clear. You're not gay?'

'No.'

'But the constant references to genitals and rectums...all those arguments with the hookers...Are you telling me that was all real?'

I nodded.

'And you're definitely not gay?'

I nodded again. And then I realised that he was.

Grayson finally took his hand off my knee.

'I really thought there was some sexual tension between us. All that stuff you wrote about me, that wasn't your repressed sexuality?'

I handed him the joint. 'I'm in a relationship with Lara. We're having sex.' Just to make sure, I put my thumb and forefinger together to form a ring, then poked the finger on my right hand in and out of the circle a few times. 'That's her fanny,' I said. 'Not her bum.'

Grayson took another drag. 'Thanks for the biology lesson, that's really cleared up a lot of confusion for me.' He blew out the smoke. 'Look, I would like it if none of this gets repeated. I'm still not ready to go public. That's why I wanted a few pictures of me and Lara together, to make it seem as if we were attracted to each other. It's probably also why Lara doesn't want to be seen with you…because…you know.'

I didn't. But that whole you know, I know thing, was just too confusing right now. And so, we finished putting a big fat one in our mouths, then walked back, just not hand in hand. Everyone else was on set. I took the bottle of rum and poured a very large one. Everything seemed like an innuendo. I drank it and drank another.

By the time I was drunk I also had the munchies. The canteen area was in darkness. Judging by the sound coming from their tents, I doubt if the hookers were going to have any time to cook for me unless I paid them. I needed cake. I stumbled around until found a sponge slice. Then Eve appeared. As I have said before, she is quite fit. Curvy, mid-thirties, flirty, a sort of busty British Mrs Robinson for the Maxim generation. And she wore the big red lipstick. The phrase *MILF* had not yet been invented, but I think she helped create it. I was clearly too far gone to go all the way back to the jungle and into my tent. She knew the hookers would eat me alive, and not in a good dirty way. She took me back to her tent. Like all good actors, I took her bed and she slept in another tent with the make up artist.

When I awoke, Eve had already gone to the costume hut. I felt like a bag of shit. Having looked at myself in the mirror, all I could do was point and say, 'There is a man.' When I stepped out of the tent a line of film crew staff was walking past. I got cheers and whistles. They thought I had gone from sleeping with cat girl to having sex with a cougar. Anyone with any decency and integrity would have immediately defended the woman's honour and told the men they were wrong. Instead, I raised my fist as if having scored in the world cup final. After being mistaken for a closet homosexual, would it really be too bad to let these poor men think I was a stud?

Thirty-two

Among the crowd of extras, hardly anyone noticed a new creature. It had a sort of donkey mask, with large ears and teeth. What was noticeable was that this extra always stayed in the background and always kept his mask on during the breaks. I sneaked off with Cameron to smoke a joint.

'Who's the goofy fuck. The one that looks like the Freddie Mercury slept with Mr Ed?'

'That's John Kurtis, the old director,' said Cameron as he took off his Ape mask. 'He sneaked back onto the set. None of the executives can know he's here. The make-up unit stitched together one of Charlton Heston's old toupees and a set of Steve Buscemi's false teeth.'

I looked over at this dreamlike vision.

'Did they also give him the large donkey penis that's swinging between his legs?'

Cameron shook his head. 'I don't know where he got that from? He's hiding in the jungle.'

'What's he going to do?'

Cameron shrugged. 'He's going to cast a spell on the film so that it flops harder than that massive dong between his legs.

Jesus. No one is ever going to let their kids see this if he's in the background.'

As Jane Dough had merely been given a call sheet with extras listed as either Wokners or Borlocks, she didn't bother to look to see what sort of creatures they were. In some ways the production was forming into similar tribes as the book. The film crews were at the very bottom. The technical crews slightly higher up. We the actors were the same as the characters in the book, seemingly distrusted by everyone. And then you had the few at the top, the lead actors and the executives. Put into this mix a donkey acting as the author, and I knew a revolution was coming (hopefully not the donkey as well).

#

Another morning. Makeup was done within thirty minutes; enough time for me to drink my iced skinny mocha latte. The hookers had noticed how many people now said "Hello" to me and decided that I must be important. Kincaid sat in the chair next to me and stared at his reflection in the mirror.

'I have a magnificent head for wigs. Shame it took so long for something like that to come to fruition. Johnny Depp was twenty-one when he got his first big break, Lee Harvey Oswald was twenty-four when he got his.' Kincaid put in his

contact lens. 'I suppose I should be grateful to have had a life before fame. Be careful you don't end up like Ozymandias.'
I blew the ripples across my coffee.

'The lead singer of Black Sabbath?'
Kincaid nodded. 'Might of well have been. Seize the day, dear buy; seize the day.'
I left, seizing a doughnut on my way out.

I had another meeting with Artie Fufkin, Pollywood Productions. Artie was a nice guy, but he had no imagination, and a twitch that made his head jerk to the side every couple of seconds.

'The rushes are looking great,' said Artie. 'But we need to focus on your image. Try to be a bit more assertive in every shot. It's too late to reshoot all your scenes; so, we are going to do a couple of photo shoots with you still in costume, laughing with the extras, talking to Brandon, that sort of thing.' As he twitched, the doughnut he was holding was squeezed so hard, a blob of jam came out and landed on the cat.
I didn't care.

'Any news about the Star Wars film?
Artie's head jerked towards his shoulder.

'George Lucas is going to direct. He wants a British actor to play Obi and is going to film quite a bit in England. Didn't you have an uncle that worked at Elstree film studios? George loves all that everything's connected stuff.'

I nodded and gave a little twitch as well.

'He also did a bit on The Shining and The Empire Strikes back.'

Artie nodded sideways.

'You need to get that story perfected when we do the chat show circuit. It might even work if they are looking for other British actors. They always play great bad guys.'

I could see myself on a sofa in a galaxy far, far, away.

'What about any other parts?'

'The boy playing Darth Vader is also going to have a sidekick,' Artie replied. 'Jar Jar Binks, and he could end up being the biggest star in the film.'

I grabbed Artie, almost getting hit by his head.

'That's the role I was born to play. Jar Jar Binks sounds like he could be the new Han Solo.'

Artie nodded in agreement (I think). 'More news on the Lord of the Rings film. New Line are now making it a trilogy. You get signed up for one, you get paid for three.' The quicker he walked, the more his head snapped.

'I don't know,' I replied. 'Fantasy has sort of had its day. We've got Sal Klimer's Owlman, George Clooney is doing a new Batman film. Is anyone really going to watch another comic book hero or wizard in a few years' time?'

And there, dear readers, is the fuck up we all make in life. I had a money man talking to me about art; and me, the portrait of an artist as a young man, talking business, with the key factor that neither of us knew what the fuck we were talking about.

I was to find out later that whilst I was playing God, Jane Dough was playing politics. The *Island of Dr Farquar's Fiends* was originally going to be a low budget psychological horror thriller, with the themes of propaganda and genetics being at the forefront. When Brandon Farlow and Sal Klimer came on board, the budget trebled, mostly on salaries. The studio sets became a real island. It all sounded great on paper. But movies are shot on film.

Now the executives were going to set the film as a loss maker, with a view to being released purely for the academy's consideration. It might make a profit if re-released after the Oscar's, or on this new DVD thing. More importantly, if Brandon Farlow died before the film had its cinema release. The film world is that brutal.

Jane Dough was told to get the script completed no matter what especially Brandon Farlow's scenes. But Jane Dough was not an amateur. She had only agreed to take over directing the film if the studio gave her a three-picture deal. And Jane was also an artist. The idea of filming crap just wasn't in her nature. Unbeknown to me, Jane was re-shooting some of my scenes with Lara using Geno Wright.

On the way back to the costume hut I was stopped by a sound in the jungle.

'Psst.'

I looked up to see a donkey in a tree. As John Kurtis tried to swing down from the branches, a foot long rubber penis kept hitting me in the face.

'Hold my legs,' said Kurtis.

As I grabbed him, the donkey schlong almost poked my eye out, before coming to a flaccid rest on my shoulder. One of the hooker's walked past carrying the cat.

'First minkey, now dinkey,' she said. 'I know a lot of perverts; I used to work for Bank of England. But you bad man. You never save cat.'

Kurtis slipped down onto the ground and looked around to check the coast was clear.

'What's happening to my precious film?'

'Jane is doing a good job,' I replied. 'But she's not getting much help from the stars.' I was talking about the nights being too cloudy to film.

Kurtis grabbed my shoulder and spoke with a hushed Scottish accent.

'You're right. It's that bastard Klimer who has to pay.' He looked around again. 'I'm going to give that shit something he's never seen before. Real talent. Tell the others the battle scene is going to be glorious. They can take away my script; but they shall never take away my dignity.'

I squirmed a little.

'Your fake donkey penis is caught on my belt buckle.' Between us we managed to pull his knickers knocker free.

'Don't forget laddie, the revolution is coming. It will be Project Mayhem, with bananas.' He ran back into the jungle, shouting 'Freedom, freedom' until the rubber dong hit his knees, and he fell over a tree stump. 'Fuck it, ya snakey bastard.

Thirty-three

Maybe it's not my weekend
But it's gonna be my year.
    All Time Low, Weightlessness.

Back in England, the biggest manhunt since Kevin Costner's career went missing was taking place. Somehow, Bastad had turned me into the most wanted man in England. His enquiries abroad meant that Interpol got involved. Because my name was linked to a Hollywood production company, the CIA and the FBI flagged me as a "Person of Interest." Working in the far east, the Russians wanted to know who I was. I had become James Bond without having to ever wear a tuxedo. Airports were also informed, which made me an international terrorist. Port authorities all over the world were given pictures of me. Unfortunately, the best that Bastad could find were the promotional pictures from the youth production of Bugsy Malone. Because Bastad had never said what it was I was wanted for; I became linked to every major crime that had ever happened. It was the great rock and roll swindle. Famous for being famous. I was all hype and no talent. Rumours appeared that there was a million-pound bounty on my head. But I had no idea of how much shit I was in.

There was one radio phone. You could use the fax machine, or the new dial up internet to send an email; but I didn't know anyone that had a computer or an email address. Theses was no way of sending text messages, so rather than ringing my mate Billy Custard, I used my mobile phone to play Snake. I could have used the old-fashioned method of sending a post card.

Having a lovely time. Got drunk, got stoned, got laid. Wish you were here mum, say hello to dad.
But I couldn't be arsed. I was gutted I wasn't going to see Oasis at Knebworth with my mates, but I was already dreaming of being a bigger rock star than Liam Gallagher.

What I didn't know was that after an investigation that had already cost hundreds of thousands of pounds and had involved a thousand police officers from all over the world, Bastad had finally found out where I was. How? Well, I blame the media. After all those resources had been spent getting nowhere, he had been sitting in his dining room (in full uniform), when his wife called from the kitchen.

'Another cup of tea, chief Inspector?'
As she came in with the teapot, he turned the page of his newspaper. She put down a plate of custard creams.

'Did you read those lovely things the papers said about Tony Blair?'

Bastad stared at some pictures.

'The two faced malignant shit hole.'

His wife wasn't so sure.

'Well, the Daily Mirror called him our next prime minister. But I do wish you wouldn't quote about him from the Police Gazette.'

Bastad pointed at the paper. 'It's the little cocksucker I've been chasing for the last few weeks. He's making a bloody film with Brandon Buggering Farlow.'

And there I was in black and white. Liam Wells, the cabin boy. Stuck on an island in 1936, surrounded by a host of other actors. In 1996 Chief Inspector Bastad was ringing up for the next flight to the South Seas. A revolution was coming alright; I just didn't realise how revolting it would all end up being for me.

Thirty-four

I had read a couple of pages of *Bridget Jones Diary*. I got the bit about weighing yourself every day, counting the alcohol and cigarette intake, and keeping score. I even tried a similar version: Yesterday: Wanks, 1; cocktails, 9; joints, 4. It was a slow day. All quiet on the wanking front. I could see why the book was so popular with women. But I stopped after reading the word: *Hurrah*. Who the fuck says *Hurrah*?

I had grown up in a world of Woolworths in the high street, white dog shit in the park, and pack lunches filled with white sandwiches. When I started going to auditions, I used to get a child's ticket because I couldn't afford the adult price. And at no point did I ever look around and say "Hurrah." It was at some of these auditions that I came across people who had a totally different upbringing to me. We looked similar and were going for the same part, and so it was often down to our accents as to whether we got a call back. Was I jealous? Of course I fucking was.

These were people who went to restaurants that had more than one knife and fork next to the plate. Have another bottle of wine. No one worried about how much the bill would be. My treat as a kid was the local cafe. The one thing I remember about these posh kids is that they all had lovely hair. Both male and female all had fine clean follicles that seemed to just fall into perfect place. Since then, I have always judged how rich someone is by their hair. That's why the Royal family are at the top of the tree. They have so much money that they know they are going bald, and they don't give a fuck. My only worry was that Lara had nice hair, and one day she would see my barbershop fringe and dump me. It turned out she didn't have to wait long for me to lose my head.

It started with a simple joke between me and Cameron. He liked to go camping in the New Forest, in a place called Sandy Balls. I then proceeded to tell Cameron that I liked to bang Lara on the beach. At this point I should have remembered that Dave Dolly Grip had a video camera with night vision capabilities, especially when Cameron suggested that I should get Lara to dress up as a cat the next time I'm getting the weasel greased.

Now, in my defence, I've said before that I did not know that the new director Jane Dough was re shooting all the scenes that I had done with Lara and replacing me with Geno Wright to see how it would all work out in the edit. Let's remember that Lara certainly knew this; and she knew it every time we held hands or kissed on set, and all the times we spent on the beach. On the other hand, I had no idea what was going to happen next. So technically… technically, I am a victim here as well. Remember that.

One night we headed down to the beach with some frozen margaritas and a set of cat ears. We knew that from about ten o'clock most people would be in bed, and certainly not walking around the island unless they had a torch. Lara took off her clothes and put on the cat ears. I gazed in wonder as the moon highlighted every curve on her young body. The way she moved was like a luxury sports car changing gears. Just fucking beautiful. We soon got down to business. As usual, I was magnificent with my love sausage (look, if you want literature, go out and buy *Lady Chatterley's Lover*).

I continued to go for it, until Lara let out a loud scream.

'Get off. I've got cramp. My legs have gone numb.'
If it had ended here, it would have been a wonderful story to tell our children. Unfortunately, it didn't. As Lara tried to stand up, she noticed a small red light.

'What's that?'
Cameron fell out of a Yewtree with a camera in his hand.

'I was trying to film a giant clam,' he said.

'You fucking creep.' Lara took of the cat ears. 'Do you enjoy watching other people have sex?'

'Yes,' Cameron replied.

If he had ended there, it would have been a wonderful story to tell at our wedding. But he didn't. 'Liam told me you didn't really start until ten.'

Lara turned to me. 'How long have you been planning all this?'

'Just a few days,' said Cameron. He helpfully held up the camera. 'It took a while to get hold of this infra-red camera from Dave Golly-Grip, but once I told him what it was for, he was happy to oblige.'

Lara held out her hand. 'Give it to me.'

Cameron started to undo his sorts. 'OK, but you promise not to laugh?'

'The fucking camera,' said Lara. 'I don't care if its infra-red or intravenous, give me that fucking film.' Lara grabbed the camera, took out the small video cassette, and threw the camera onto the sand before walking back along the beach.

I turned to Cameron.

'The rest of the crew know?'

'Yes,' said Cameron. 'They were also hoping you could shag Eve as well, dressed as a sailor. Spastic Wank Nigel from rigging has even written a script.'

I had so many problems, it was a problem trying to sort them into any priority. 'What the fuck is this, Charlie Sheen's fantasy Island? Lara is never going to speak to me again, Eve is going to go ballistic if she ever finds out, the other actors will think I'm a pervert (and I'm working with Reginald Kincaid), the director will cut my part, the executives will want me kicked off the island to be sent home in disgrace, I'll lose my contract, and all my family and friends will think I'm a weirdo.'

Cameron nodded. 'Yes, it's quite a pickle.'

Personally, I was hoping the situation would just blow over, and we could all have a good laugh about it at the wrap party. I headed back to the camp. I could see Lara sitting on the beach. I hoped she wasn't going to go all Goodwill Hunting on me and have a big speech about relationships.

'I'm sorry,' I said. 'I admit I told him about us, but I honestly didn't know he was going to make a film about it.'

'But you told him about us.'

'Well, yes.'

'And that we were having sex.'

'Yes, but.'

'And where we had sex.'

'Yes, and I can see how this might look a bit bad.'

'And what time we usually did it?'

'Yes.'

'And you got me dressed as a cat just to appeal to your sordid little fantasies?'

I had a feeling we were going around in circles. Lara finally looked at me.

'Do you know what you are?'

(I was desperate to say, "A Dreamweaver?")

'You're lucky,' continued Lara. 'You don't really work hard. You never really push yourself. You never want to do anything that involves being serious just in case people might see the real you behind the mask. You were lucky to get this job by being related to the author. You were lucky to get more lines by Sal Klimer being a massive twat. And you were very lucky to get me. But I can't be with someone who lets luck make all his decisions for him. From now on, let's just be professional until the filming is over.' She handed me back the cat ears and headed back to her tent.

I stayed on the beach, feeling like I had lost all nine lives at once.

Thirty-five

The next morning, I sat with Dame Helen and Reginald as he drank his Bloody Mary, and I told them all about last night. Kincaid felt sorry for me (and himself, he was hoping to watch it on DVD). Helen told me I was a twat. Women want a man who protects them, not puts them into their own pornographic home movie.

I watched as Artie Fufkin of Pollywood Productions walked along the beach. The gentle slant of the sand caused his twitch to become more pronounced, with his ear almost hitting his shoulder. He climbed up the sloping bank towards us, his head jerking with every other step.

'Here he comes,' said Kincaid. 'The sniper's nightmare.' When Artie finally arrived at the bar, I noticed one ear was more sunburnt that the other. He shook hands with Kincaid.

'Hi. Artie Fufkin, Pollywood Productions.'

'Reginald Kincaid. Pleasantly pissed.'

Artie had some big news for me. 'There are auditions coming up for a London gangster film, "Lock Stock." That could be the part just made for you.'

I shrugged. 'I thought I would be based in Hollywood by the time this film comes out?'

'But this film is perfect.'

Kincaid handed Artie a drink, with a straw. 'Tell me Artie, how did you end up as a Hollywood agent?'

'My father owned one of the largest casting companies in L.A.' Artie replied. 'Before he died of the clap.' He went for a drink, but his mouth missed the straw.

'Ah,' replied Kincaid. 'Then your mother was in showbusiness as well?'

Artie turned to me. 'I'm off to send the fax to George Lucas about you having a family connection at Elstree Studios.'

I shook my head. 'Don't, I want my talent to get me the part.'

I heard Dame Helen laugh. 'Don't be so bloody stupid. You can't change the past, so just move on and keep going. If you want something that's important, then you need to do the work.

On that note I walked down to the canteen.

It wasn't so much the film crew; it was the smiles on the hooker's faces that made me nervous. At some point I would have to go to the costume hut and see Eve, preferably before she had spoken to Lara. The only good thing was that the film industry is filled with warm hearted lovable people who were always willing to forgive and help others when they had messed up.

Thirty-six

Chief Inspector Bastad walked through the tropical airport wearing a straw trilby, mesh polo shirt, and extremely tight shorts. The outfit gave him the air of a seasoned pervert from 1976. His bulbous testicles seemed to have expanded proportionally to the shrinkage of his nob. Bastad polished off the look with white socks and brown sandals. He had his warrant card, and a bum bag of loose change, as he didn't like to give foreigners too much money. He found a payphone and rung headquarters.

'Hello, it's the chief inspector (he expected them to know who he was). Is Liam Wells still on Paradise Island?'

As he waited, an old man in dark glasses and a white walking stick gently tapped Bastad's holdall that had been placed on the floor, showing a new video camera inside.

'Oh, I'm dreadfully sorry to bother you,' said the blind man. 'I was wondering if you could help point me in the general direction of the disabled toilet.'

Bastad turned to him.

'Fuck off, you bloody benefit cheat. Some of us work for a living.' He turned back to the phone. 'No sign of his passport being checked in England. Good.' He looked down at his holdall. Next to the video camera was a set of handcuffs.

#

With things a bit tense between me and Lara, I struggled to be my usual jovial self at work. I knew things were bad when Sal Klinger pulled me to one side.

'Tell me, who's your agent?'

'Artie Fufkin, Pollywood Productions.'

'The Weeble? He tried to be my agent a couple of times. In the end I had to slap him to make sure he got the message. What's he getting for his ten percent?'

'The new Star Wars film.'

'What part?'

I hadn't seen the script. 'All I know is they are already talking trilogy.'

Klimer stroked his fake moustache. 'Well, you're too young to take any of my roles. I'll put you in touch with Weinstein,' said Klimer. 'He's a man with his finger in a lot if pies. Just don't outshine me on this film, otherwise you will never work in Hollywood again.'

Was he now threatening me to act badly? This wasn't a soap. 'But…'

He stepped in so close I could see the weave of his moustache. 'Just say your fucking lines and move on…if you want to stay in the picture. Oh, and by the way, don't tell anyone you are sleeping with the young actress and the costume designer on this film, I want the press to think that's me.'

When he left, I remembered that everyone now thought I was sleeping with Eve. As for Artie Fufkin, Pollywood Productions, I couldn't help feeling a bit sorry for him. This guy was like a baby lamb with a comb over compared to those wolves. The other executives would call him "Pez head" and "Linda Lovelace's love child," knowing he would never answer back. I guess all the Artie Fufkin (Pollywood Productions) and John Kurtis' of the world were the same. If you never stand up for yourself, you will never get anywhere. Did I need to be more assertive?

I soon found out. The next night I took all the rice and bread from the canteen and carried it over to Klimer's silver trailer. I covered the roof with wet rice and breadcrumbs, turning it into a giant smorgasbord. When Klimer came back from shooting he didn't notice anything was wrong. Only the hookers cat showed any interest. But come the dawn, every bird within a twenty-mile radius of the island headed towards a free breakfast. They landed in silence, then their beaks hit the roof like machine guns.

Klimer woke up screaming. He thought Kurtis was wanking himself to death on the roof. When he tried to get out, I had pushed a broom against the door. I had an early morning meeting with Artie, so we just happened to be there. When Klimer looked out of the window, all he saw was us, and in the distance a deranged Donnie Darko type donkey waving a bag of rice at him with one hand and holding a bazooka sized penis with the other. Poor Klimer didn't know if he was going to get fed or fucked. Which was ironic because of what happened next.

A young hooker climbed out of the window. As she put a leg out, I wondered about the price of bananas. She was wearing a devil's costume. Then a second hooker climbed out, wearing an angel's outfit. Her wings made it difficult to get out of the gap. She was also wearing a white thong. On each arse cheek was one half of Klimer's moustache. No wonder his middle finger always smelled funny. As she jumped down, Klimer looked out of the window.

'Who did this? Who did this?' What he saw was Artie Fufkin of Pollywood Productions snapping his head, Klimer realised what was going on. 'You did it with Kurtis,' he said. 'I know you, Artie fucking Fufkin.'

'Of Pollywood Productions,' said Artie. Before denying any involvement, he cranked his neck to the side.

The other executives who had been watching, having no idea if Fufkin was involved or not, suddenly had a new-found respect for this little nutcracker.

Klimer climbed out of the window, naked, and fell to the ground. The birds, believing he was a human worm, they went for him. The hookers' cat, having spent the morning trying to climb up the roof, suddenly saw its chance at targets much lower down. Klimer ran screaming into the jungle.

'I hope he's OK,' I said.

'Fuck him,' replied Fufkin of Pollywood Productions. One of the executives came over.

'Nobody will believe this.'

'Yes, they will,' replied Cameron. He held up the video camera. 'We can watch this as many times as we want.' Cameron wasn't the brightest bulb in the house. He thought the fallopian tubes were on the London underground. And although he may not have been as good as Hitchcock, that day he certainly got a close-up on one.

Thirty-seven

Where were you while we were getting high?
    Oasis, Champagne supernova.

After the sailors had gone missing, me, as young Jack Bates, and Kincaid as Captain Rimlick, now with a good eye but still wearing sunglasses, went through the jungle looking for them. We spotted Monty heading towards the village and followed him. Diddler used the horn of Diabolos to call the Borlocks into the centre of the village, and they were injected again. This time they were helping to inject the stuff into each other's anus. There were also quite a few drinking the serum straight from the bottle. Monty tried to maintain order.
Grayson: 'I need some Borlocks to try something different. No, not that again. This is a chance for some of you to end up at the white house.'
Tango stepped forward. The orangutan was now wearing a baggy shirt and sporting a large orange afro hairdo.
Tango: 'You have told that to us before.'
Grayson: 'You can speak again?

Tango: I have watched you playing with my Borlocks. You have kept us in ignorance, just to make your life better. Our sins were caused by you. And now you tell us that the only way we will rise to the top is by putting everyone else down. But you, and all those at the white house, you will always have the real power.'

Grayson: 'No. We are doing all this for you. Of course, times are hard, for you; and things will get harder, for you. But I promise, that once I have total power, everyone will be better off.'

Tango: 'You have kept us in the dark for long enough. The time has come for change.' He held out the Zippo lighter.

The Borlocks clapped out messages as Grayson limped back on the golf cart. He could only save himself by throwing the rest of the bottles of serum on the ground. Diddler drove the mobility scooter towards the white house shouting 'Klatu Birada Nicto.'

Whilst watching these events from the jungle someone came up behind me.

Captain Rimlick: 'Don't take my wallet. Oh, it's you Lawton. Just getting used to my eyesight. What are you doing here?'

Geno: 'Lola made me come.'

Lara stepped up behind him, wearing a catsuit, glancing at me.

Lara: 'The rest of your crew have all been taken. Dr Farquar took them into Wokners.'

We listened to the creatures clapping.

Lara: 'The Borlocks are messaging each other. They are going to destroy the white house tonight. And they are also going to stop you from leaving the island.'

Kincaid: 'Jack, you must get to the white house and take Lady Ruffsnatch to the boat straight away. But you will need to get past all those creatures hitting their hands together.'

Me: 'You mean you want me to run like the clappers, captain?'

Kincaid: 'Yes boy. But be as quick as you can.'

I ran into the jungle, pretending to be one of the Borlocks. Lara took hold of Geno's arm.

Lara: 'You must use my back passage. I can take you to laboratory.'

   I did a few more running shots with the assistant director. Pushing palm leaves out of the way, out of breath, sweating, clapping, until I got to the white house. To say I was wooden would be an understatement. All I could think about was Lara. Why was she now with Geno? We had already filmed my scene with Lady Ruffsnatch, as it was meant to be Arlen Parker who had found us in the jungle; but everyone was still on the set. Cut.

#

I found Lara hanging around the village.
 'You seem to be getting pretty friendly with Geno?'
She kept walking. 'And you've been ignoring me since you got told about the Star Wars film. Why don't you go speak to Eve about it? We've only got a few more scenes left Liam. Let's not blow it.'
I walked away. But when the next time someone tells you about subtext, just remember what she said.

Thirty-eight

There was going to be a screening of a film tonight to celebrate the last few days of filming. It was a sort of wrap party before we wrapped. I was the last one in the costume tent. Eve looked at me.

'Trouble in Paradise?'

I nodded. Eve gave me a sad smile. 'Grayson? Don't worry, he told me there was a thing between him and you and that Lara was happy to be a beard.'

I was still not sure why people thought Lara had a beard. She had whiskers. I played along, hoping another woman would have the answer to my problem.

'Now its Geno.'

I stopped when a few extras came in.

'Don't worry,' said Eve. 'This will be our little secret.'

Looking back, Eve thought I was talking about one thing, I thought she was talking about another, while the rest of the island thought it was something totally different. If I knew how to be more articulate and be able to speak about my feelings, it would have saved a lot of pages.

#

When I reached base camp, I went straight to the bar. Kincaid poured me a margarita

'Have you re-shot some scenes without me?' I asked. Kincaid poured himself another drink.

'Every director is different. Jane wants to use the black and white to make it more of a film noir, showing the dichotomy of those who have and those who have not.'
I thought Kincaid was waffling.

'Lara seems to be on set all the time lately. Where is she now?'
Kincaid looked through the palm trees at the second camp.

'I would go check her tent myself,' he said. 'But I've walked in on Lara getting changed at least seventeen times now, and I think she suspects me to be a bit of a pervert.' He finished his drink. 'I believe she's with Geno and Jane rehearsing tomorrows scene.' He buttoned up his shirt. 'We going to watch the midnight screening of "Island of Lost Souls." You coming?'

'Janes asked me to look at the last act to see what needs editing out,' I lied.

After finishing another margarita, I could see a light inside Kincaid's tent. I went in to turn it off. The bed, table and wardrobe all looked untouched. Had the old rascal been spending all his nights with the hooker's? There were a few books. *The Island of Dr Farquars Fiends,* looked like an old copy he had bought from a charity shop. *Lord of the Rings, The Fellowship of the Ring*, and *Journey's End* both looked like Kincaid had owned them since the sixties, *Brave New World, Lord of the Flies*. I had read *Lord of the Flies* at school. I picked it up. *"The thing is – fear can't hurt you any more than a dream."* That may have been true for a group of kids stuck on an island, but when it comes to being in love with someone who doesn't love you back, fear and dreams are the same thing. I closed the book, turned off the light, and walked out of the tent.

Grayson was at the bar. I poured him a drink.

'Look,' I said. 'I'm sorry we got off on the wrong foot. It's just that I really fancied Lara, and I thought you were after her as well.'

'I heard you screwed it up,' Grayson replied. 'Not literally. I am planning to come out once I've become big enough not to get cancelled. I thought the reason you didn't like me was a class thing?'

I poured myself another drink. 'Lara told me I was the sort of man who had spent his life relying on luck to get to get here. If that's the case, how come I feel like shit?'

Grayson told me about his life. Bullied at a posh school for being different, falling out with his father because he wanted him to go into the family business rather than waste his time with art, finding himself at university through studying drama. And then the irony of being turned down for parts because he sounded too posh. When he did get on set, the crew would avoid him because they thought he was a snob. It seems that the past keeps coming back no matter what you do.

'Sometimes I think it's my bloody hair,' he said. 'They give you a special shampoo at Eton, that's why some of the teachers have large right hands.'

If Grayson had said nothing else, we could have walked to the canteen area blissfully unaware of what was about to unfold. But he never.

'I thought you would have been on set tonight. Jane is directing scene forty-two again, the one with you and Lara in the courtyard.' He said it with a smile, then realised I didn't know anything about it. 'She came and offered me the love interest, but I said you would have the better storyline with Lara. I thought Jane or Lara would have told you?'

If I had been living solely on luck, it was beginning to turn bad. I wondered if that bloody cat had anything to do with it. Grayson raised his glass.

'To success, even if we have helped someone else to get it.' I drank the bitter fruit of victory. No, not really. There's no point ending another chapter with some more fake pearls of wisdom. I drank because I felt as if I had been shafted. I had gone from writing myself as the hero in the first draft of the script, to becoming a minor character in my own bloody film. This is not how I expected the last act to turn out.

Thirty-nine

I sat at a picnic table in the middle of the jungle as Grayson, Kincaid and Dame Helen laughed and joked about all the disastrous auditions they had attended. From Kincaid singing "Yummy, yummy, yummy I've got love in my tummy" when he went for the part of Kane in *Alien*, to Dame Helen reading *The Tale of Peter Rabbit* for what turned out to be *Fatal Attraction*. I was more concerned about Lara, and the fact that both she and Geno were still missing in action. As one of the hookers bent over to clear away the plates, I got a glimpse of Klimer's fake moustache and wondered where he was as well? The jungle at night was hot and sweaty, like my balls. Beyond the lights and the music was a darkness filled with strange sounds and strange eyes staring back. Where was Lara?

As a tribute to the Oasis concert at Knebworth I was missing, Kincaid invented a drink of sparkling wine, Limoncello, and gin, which he called the "Champagne Supernova." How the old soak knew about Oasis was a mystery to me. Most people I knew over forty only bought a CD player just so they could buy their vinyl albums over again. But Kincaid seemed to know all about Brit Pop. He liked buying records. He also told me that time is a flat circle, so I think the drugs were working. I was also keeping an eye out for Lara, hoping to tell her how I was feeling. Kincaid took my hand.

'Please Liam, don't look back in anger.'

Very witty, very droll. I had a suspicion that everyone had been acting strangely around me (and some of them were even wooden at that) because they knew Lara was sleeping with Geno. But they didn't want to tell me because of my erratic behaviour, frightened that I might leave the island. They might have been right. I had gone into the jungle to make a big budget movie. We had everything we wanted. But there were too many people wanting to be the star. There was too much money. We had access to too much drink and drugs. And little by little I had slowly gone insane. This was like Butlins with the Borgia's.

We moved to the clearing. A projector light shone onto a silver screen. Jane Dough was going to show *The Island of Lost Souls*; a 1932 film starring Charles Laughton. The book had Dr Farquar as a slim man, like a cigarette; but both old and new films portrayed him similar in shape and size to a steamed pudding. When I realised that directors would often put things in films as metaphors for something else that they believed in, I wondered what this meant? Perhaps it was the idea that those who played God quickly lost their sense of moderation? Or it could have just been that a fat actor was available at the time.

I had already seen this old film. After searching through Sight and Sound and Empire Magazine, I came across a VHS video copy for sale in one of those back page's adverts. They wanted fifty pounds for it. Fuck me. The hookers were cheaper. But I suppose this was 1996, you couldn't stream it, nor make a copy and put it on a memory stick. The advert said that it was a pre code production, which meant that it was before the Hayes code. That was the era when a minority decided what the majority should be allowed to see and hear. A film like this could show a bit more skin (for 1932), the good guys could be a little bit bad, and the bad guys be a little bit good. It also meant that ideas such as treating people like animals could be portrayed in ways that would make the audience think. As such, this particular film had been banned in England until 1958, the same year America sent a monkey into space.

The *Island of Lost Souls* didn't have a young Jack the cabin boy in it. I suppose that should have been a warning; but I was so pissed on Champagne Supernova's I honestly expected to see myself in the background. My aim was to carry on drinking until I couldn't see anything; but then I saw Geno and Lara walking out of the jungle laughing and joking with the director Jane Dough.

I saw Cameron arrive and grab a bottle of lager.

'Have you been filming Geno and Lara?'

Cameron lit a joint.

'Yeah. It's going pretty well.'

'The sex, or just filming?'

It seemed like a straightforward question. But I could see Cameron struggle to answer it.

'This stuff is a lot stronger than last time. I think I prefer it from the shell. The spirals. Did you know the spiral inside a shell-'

I stopped him. 'Is there something going on that I don't know about?

Cameron took another drag.

'I heard you was with Eve the other night. I bet it's like stroking a dolphin's nose, all wet and smooth. Is she willing to be a bit more experimental?'

'Forget Eve,' I said. 'What else has been going on?'

'But it must be nice. A woman of that age can probably do a bit more of the heavy lifting when it comes to foreplay.'

'Yes, yes. Sex with Eve is great. The only problem I have is brushing my teeth afterwards. Now what about my question?'

'You're sleeping with Eve?' Lara stared at me. She had appeared from nowhere like a female sex assassin (a vaginja?) Geno also appeared and decided to put his nose in.

'You're sleeping with Eve, the lady in the costume department?'

Lara stood in front of me. 'When did this start happening?'

'It might have been before you,' said Cameron. 'So, technically, you would be the side chick. But let's not start jumping to conclusions and using the phrase, "sexy slut."'

'When did you start having sex with Liam?' Geno asked Lara.

Cameron kept the conversation going. 'If I hadn't dropped my camera when I fell out of the tree, I could have showed you.' said Cameron.

'You filmed it?'

'Look,' I said. 'None of this is as bad as it seems.'

'You got drunk and masturbated in an airplane toilet,' said Lara. 'You tried to kill a monkey with a coconut after you tried to have sex with a cat. You defecated in a golf cart. A cook caught you playing with a donkey's dong. You got your friend to film us having sex with me dressed as a cat, and you're going through the costume department like a sewing machine, What the hell are you doing here?'

'I'm just trying to make a movie,' I replied.

'I'd watch it,' said Cameron.

Geno decided to escort Cameron into the jungle. Lara shook her head.

'How could you.' She kept shaking her head like a female Fufkin (Pollywood Productions). 'I really felt we had something, and all this time you were also having sex with Eve.'

'Who was?' Eve appeared.

I raised my hands. 'For fucks sake. Doesn't anyone knock in this place?'

Eve was clearly not in the mood for jokes.

'Whose been saying I've had vaginal intercourse with someone?'

Cameron called out from the jungle.

'In Liam's defence, he's always been too much of a gentleman to say if it was anal sex as well.'

Lara pointed at me. 'Apparently, Liam has been telling everyone that you are one of his conquests.'

'I never actually said those lines,' I replied. 'People saw me coming out of your tent the other morning, and they all thought we had done something.'

'And you told them the truth?' Eve asked me.

'I tried,' I said. 'But it was the film crew, and the cook had made sausage rolls.' I knew everyone would see past that lie straight away.

Lara now turned to Eve. 'He spent the night with you?'

'The poor boy was almost in tears,' said Eve. 'But of course, nothing happened. He's gay.'

This was a surprise to everyone listening, including me, and the large group of cast and crew members that had decided this was more interesting than the film and were all standing nearby.

'Fucking hell,' said big Dave Dolly Grip.

Lara turned back to me.

'You're gay?'

'I heard him,' said Eve. 'He was speaking to another man the other night, explaining what it was like to be gay. I felt sorry for the poor dear.'

'Is that why we only did it in the dark,' Lara asked me. 'And you wanted me to dress as a cat?'

Cameron came back.

'And why you were playing with the pendulous plastic penis on a man dressed as a donkey?'

'Fucking hell,' said Dave Dolly Grip.

I didn't know whether the audience were shocked or impressed?

'It wasn't a real donkey; it was John Kurtis. And he caught his penis in my belt buckle, so I helped him release it.'

A Hollywood executive, who had seen and heard a lot worse, could only say.

'John Kurtis is still on the island?'

Dave Dolly Grip raised his eyebrows. 'Fucking hell.'

Back to Lara.

'You gave the director a hand job to get more lines?'

'Fucking hell.'

I turned to my left. 'Will you just focus on the film, Dave Dolly Grip.' I turned to my right. 'No,' I said to Lara. 'No one got a hand job, blow job, or even a rim job. This isn't Weinstein's Island.'

Lara hadn't taken her eyes off me. 'But you did have a conversation with another man about being gay?'

'Yes.'

'Are you gay?'

'No.'

'So, if you're not gay, then the other man is?'

I had been raised with that white working-class value that you didn't let your mates down. I now considered Grayson my friend (although if anyone was in desperate need of a nickname, it was him) and I wasn't going to grass him up. Lara asked another question.

'Who was the other man?'

Hang on, I suddenly thought to myself. I haven't been having sex with Eve; but Lara was the one spending all her time with Geno. Even worse, Geno could have a massive cock, and afterwards she would whisper those sweet words in his ear "you're so much bigger than Liam," wasn't doing me any favours. Why should she be the one getting to ask all the questions?

'I've got just as much right to a private life as you,' I said. And if I had stopped there, it might have been a dignified end to what had been a melodramatic evening. But I never. 'Even though you're now sleeping with Geno.'

To some of the crew, this production appeared to be nothing but a den of depravity and debauchery; filled with insane lust and sinful perversions. So, they were not really surprised. Dave Dolly Grip slowly whispered, 'Fucking hell.' Lara acted surprised.

'What are you going on about?'
Now I had her.

'Oh, don't act all surprised. All those times you and Geno were out late pretending to do extra scenes; no one works that hard on a film set.' After giving my acceptance speech, I was just about to walk away, when I had one more person to thank. 'Do you know what, it doesn't matter. I just wish you'd told me you were shagging Geno after Sal Klimer tried to have sex with you.'

Dave Dolly Grip held up a placard. On it was written, *fucking hell.*

I honestly thought I had won. If Lara had walked away, I would have been left in blissful ignorance, secure in the knowledge that I had been right. But she never.

'You really don't have a clue, do you?' (See, I told you.) 'Has no one else told you?' She kept staring. 'Reggie, Dame

Helen, even that cock womble Cameron must have realised something was going on?'

'Hey,' said Cameron's voice in the jungle. 'Uncalled for, lady.'

I looked at Reginal Kincaid. I looked at Dame Helen. Nothing stayed secret on the island for very long. My late-night drunken wanks had become so legendary that they now had to be included in the production schedule. But something was being kept hidden from me. Kincaid looked over at Jane Dough but said nothing. Now I was really lost.

Lara gave me a smile that reminded me of the air hostesses when they are saying goodbye to the middle-aged men as they get off the plane.

'The thing is.' Lara paused. 'It was agreed.' Another pause (come on love, you're not trying to hold in a fart on a first date). 'That your scenes would be re shot with Geno saying your lines just in case the producers felt it would make a better film.'

It took a moment for me to process the information. Better film? Above me, the screen played *The Island of Lost Souls*, and I knew exactly what they meant.

'Geno is playing Jack the cabin boy?'

'No,' said Lara. 'He's still Lawton. But Jane wanted to see if the love interest between me and him might also work. You would still be in the film, but just as simple Jack the cabin boy.'

This was too much. 'So, I've been doing all this work, writing new scenes, getting you more lines, and all the time you knew I would go end up on screen as the simple servant?'

Cameron clicked his fingers. 'Retard. Now I know who the producers were talking about.'

All eyes were on me.

'And you and Geno stayed silent all this time?'

Lara grabbed my arm.

'It's not Geno's fault. He said you should have been told from the start. So did Reggie. But Jane thought your acting would be better if you didn't know you were in competition and promised us all to be quiet.'

I wasn't having that.

'Come on; I'm only here because I lied about being related to the author.' I turned to my audience. 'And what a piece of work you fucking lot are. Delighting in my misery. You know what. It doesn't matter if I was in love with a man or a woman. I thought you were my friends. I guess I was wrong.' I turned to Lara. 'Well thanks for all the acting tips, and I hope I passed the audition.'

Lara knew I would probably never work in Hollywood again. She stopped me.

'If you must know, not that it's any of your bloody business, I haven't been sleeping with Geno. We haven't had sex at all.'
Now I laughed. 'All those times when you went off and I thought it may have been Grayson, Klimer, or Geno. You're telling me it was for filming?'
Lara shook her head. 'No. It was for Jane.'
Now I thought I understood. 'Geno's having sex with the director?'
Lara stepped closer. 'No, I am.'

('Fucking hell.')

'I'm the one sleeping with Jane,' continued Lara. 'After sleeping with you I decided to have sex with the female director.'
For a moment the whole island went quiet.

'Fucking Hell,' said the whole film crew.

Lara went off into the jungle. The hookers stared at me. They had finally met a man who's lovemaking was so bad he could actually turn you into a lesbian. I went back and sat at the table as Kincaid made me another Champagne Supernova, this one with plenty of ice. God, I missed having sex with Lara. I looked back up at the black and white film playing on the screen.

'Well, I've had better nights out.' I then looked at my friends. 'Why didn't any of you say something?'

'What would be the point?' Dame Helen replied. 'Being famous is not the same as being an artist. I think if you had been told your scenes were going to be cut, you would have flounced off the island and ruined it for everyone involved in the production. You needed to mature as an actor and take some responsibility first.'

The others all seemed to agree.

'No. I mean about Lara sleeping with Jane.'

'Even I didn't spot that,' said Dame Helen. 'And I've been fingered more times than a cream cake at a fat kids birthday party. Although I must say, well done when it came to sticking up for your friend.'

Kincaid and Grayson kept telling me how good I had been in my scenes. There are times when you need to just do your best even though you have no idea if it's all going to end up on the cutting room floor. I suppose they were right. The producers couldn't get rid of me now because it was not part of the script; and if they tried to edit me out later, so what. At least I could say that I was there, and I did my best. The old film continued to play out on the screen. Chances are most of the cast are dead now. But I could still see them up there, from the main players to the extras, living on as long as someone wanted to watch them. The holiday was over. It was time to get to work.

Forty

I sat alone on the beach. The stars filled the sky. I haven't got a clue about their names, the science names, not the fortune teller stuff. There must have been a hundred thousand above me. I knew I was looking at their light from a hundred years ago. Ahead of me was the ocean. If I was to start going forward, I might not see another person for a thousand miles, sitting on their own little island. The waves came up the beach. Every grain of sand that I had touched had now moved to another position on the beach or perhaps had even been taken back into the darkness of the sea. It was 1996, but it could have been a hundred years ago.

    I had started all this because of a lie. I moved to something bigger because of another lie, then ended up losing what I loved because of a lie. And every time I thought I had got it made; it was because I was too afraid to turn and face the real me. I thought I could hide from the truth. But eventually it found me. And it turned out I feared the truth more than I feared the lies. I wondered how much the others must have seen me as the faker, playing the part of someone whose whole life is just an act. In the words of David Bowie, I needed to make some changes.

I could have been with a hundred thousand other lost souls as Oasis stood on the stage and sang Champagne Supernova. Where were you while we were getting high? I was here mate, about to lose the best job I ever had and packed off home to never work in the industry again. I had well and truly fucked things up. The Darth Vader of fuck ups. The Lord of the Rings of…I stopped. I couldn't even finish my own fuck ups. That was the story of my life.

Kincaid joined me on the beach. He sat down, lit a joint, had a few puffs, then handed it to me.

'Do you remember when I told you about the audition when I gave the speech from Hamlet. I have always remembered the correct words. "I have of late, but wherefore I know not, lost all my mirth, and indeed it goes so heavily with my disposition, that this goodly frame the earth seems to me a sterile promontory; this most excellent canopy the air, look you, this mighty o'rehanging firmament, this majestical roof fretted with golden fire; why, it appeareth nothing to me but a foul and pestilent congregation of vapours. What a piece of work is a man, how noble in reason, how infinite in faculties, how like an angel in apprehension, how like a God! The beauty of the world, paragon of animals; and yet to me, what is this quintessence of dusk. Man delights not me, no, nor women neither, nor women neither."

He let the waves pass.

'Do you know what has always amazed me? Not, how did Shakespeare write all that when he was stoned? But the fact that there were people hundreds of years ago suffering from the same problems and doubts that you are going through now.'

I felt like crying.

'The thing is Reg, how can I ever go home again? All I wanted was to be someone, to get famous just so I could help all my family and my mates. I need to be famous enough so that no one would have to worry about stuff like money again. I just never thought I would have to hurt people to get there. This acting lark was meant to be my dream. So how did the normality of life get so fucked up?'

Kincaid turned to me.

'It all passes, dear boy. Want and need are two different things. All these feelings that you are going through, the things that you think you want, they will eventually fade away like those stars. The things you need will always be changing like the sand at our feet. But you are here, right now. It's up to you to stand your ground, to be a good person, to help others, and to be who you really are.'

I listened to the waves as they broke, shifting back the sand before they disappeared.

'But what if this was my moment?' I said.

'What if its mine,' Kincaid replied. 'What if the next audition and the next film is going to be my moment. The one thing you need if you want to make a career from something you love, is to be professional. As an actor people are expecting you to turn up and play the part, whether it's for the first time or the twentieth time, the lead role of one line. It doesn't matter if you are going to win an Oscar or not. The most you can do is find the truth of your own art. As for time, enjoy your youth Liam, because moments like these will never come again. Anyway, fame is not all it's cracked up to be. I should know, I've been on Celebrity Supermarket Sweep.'

I let the waves roll over my feet. They sank slightly was the water tried to escape.

'I remember doing the play *Our Day Out*,' I said. 'Where a group of kids from a run-down school were taken on a trip to the beach. There was a scene where we stopped at a zoo, and I watch a bear walk up and down its cage. I asked the teacher if the bear knew it was trapped. The teacher replied that it had been born in captivity, and so it wouldn't know anything different than a cage. If it escaped it wouldn't know how to survive. I believed it knew there was another world out there. It hadn't seen it and couldn't describe it; but something inside of that creature knew there was another place where it was free. Now I realise, I'm the fucking bear.'

Kincaid looked up at the stars.

'The only cage is in your head. You play one part, give it your best shot, and the result is a mess. You play another part, you think its rubbish, and it's the biggest hit in years. You didn't know that beforehand, so you couldn't have changed anything at the time. And in the future when asks if you would you go back and do it all again the same way, you would probably say yes. You see, none of it matters.'

I knew he was probably just trying to make me feel better. You don't get to be old without making a lot of mistakes. I suppose if you are still happy at his age then you must have got a few things right as well.

'Reg. I'm not related to the guy who wrote this book. I wouldn't know T.B. Wells if he came over and kicked me up the arse.'

Kincaid nodded. 'I knew all along.'

Somehow it didn't surprise me.

Kincaid swirled the ice cubes in his glass and finished his drink.

'I think your performance of Jim Bates the cabin boy is good enough to stay in the picture.' He poured the ice cubes onto the sand. 'Or it was until you started playing for the camera rather than playing the character.' He stood up. 'By the way, Grayson said "Thank You". He would have come here himself, but he didn't want to be seen by any reporters.'

I stood up.

'You knew he was gay?'

'Of course,' Kincaid replied. 'It was obvious from the moment I met him. It's the hair. You, on the other hand, dear boy, spend all your time staring at women as if you have just been released from prison.' Kincaid looked up at the stars. 'Come, we've a film to finish, and I need to get back for a booking on Blankety Blank.'

Forty-one

Can I take you from behind and hold you in my arms?
Happy Mondays, Bob's your Uncle.

Chief Inspector Bastad reached the main island. The small airport was in half darkness. A holiday rep came towards the group of travellers.

'Ladies and gentlemen, we are so sorry about the delay. A blind man somehow ended up on the runway and held up the planes for a few hours. The boats to take you to your island will be here in the morning.'

Bastad showed her his warrant card.

'Is there a police station near here; and do they have a boat?'

And so it was, that under this majestical canopy of stars, a police boat was commandeered by the chief inspector. The officer who had been forced to take the boat out at night was certainly not delighted, and neither were the creatures below the water as this uniformed ferryman deliberately hit every wave, forcing his passenger to hold on for dear life. But Bastad had the smile of a madman. He was going to get his revenge, oh yes, he would get his revenge, whether it was in this world, or the next.

Forty-two

I woke up that morning feeling slightly more hungover than of late. My usual plan for any fuck up would be to lie low for a while and hope for everything to get back to normal, or at least for people to stop asking me any questions. This situation was different, it involved work. I couldn't really suck up to the female boss, as my ex-girlfriend was doing that. But I needed to get back on track with Jane Dough on a professional basis.

I wondered how I should play this out in real life. I had grown up around council estates, had the same Christmas tree every year, went to the local comprehensive school and smoked joints at the top of the playing fields. Conflict meant tops off, come on then, make a fist, and see who wants to have it. There were people in my town who saw prison as a sort of health farm. A nice break away from all the drugs, and a chance to get fit in the gym. I had never had a female boss, so I was going to have to think differently. Perhaps it was time to just be honest.

I went to the back of the white house and the barn that had been converted for on-site editing. The room was filled with screens, high-tower computers, notice boards, and projection reels. All high-tech stuff in 1996.

'Excuse me, Jane, can I have a word?'

We walked towards the canteen area.

'I just want to say, you're the director, so I'm happy to do whatever you want.' As she still hadn't said anything, so I decided to carry on. 'I'm sure Lara told you about what happened last night, and again, it's got nothing to do with me. All I want to do is play Jack the cabin boy.' I thought I had done pretty well in the apology's stakes.

'You fucked up, Liam,' said Jane as we reached the kitchen area. 'The island doesn't need two Sal Klimer's. In fact, the world doesn't even deserve one Sal Klimer. The audience wants to see someone fall in love, not behave like a Johnny jerk-off. You're lucky I don't take my top off and see if you want some. I just want you to do what I ask.'

I agreed. 'I know there are only a few more scenes left. Whatever you want, I will do it.'

She agreed. 'As for myself and Lara; you're right, it has got nothing to do with you. Chances are, she is a better player off set than both of us put together. Just keep your head and finish the film. Between you and me, right now, I've got no idea how this is all going to end.'

We parted on good terms. Now for the others.

I spoke to the film crew and told them I was sorry if I had been acting like an arsehole for the last few weeks. They told me not to worry about it, a lot of people go nuts on their first film. It was like going on your first adult holiday. Even the hookers accepted my apology. They even offered me a discount, which I thought was a nice touch. I went to Eve's tent and said sorry to her, although I meant it when I said she was fit for her age. She thanked me. As I left I noticed Geno Wrights trainers just near the bed.

    I walked back to the actor's camp. Reginald, Dame Helen, and Grayson were sitting under the shade by the bar. They all accepted my apology for not listening to what they had been trying to tell me all along. Never confuse a script with real life. I finally turned down a free drink. There were still other people I had to see. I went down to the beach. The cool breeze was refreshing. The birds glided above me, watching the water break, following the patterns, until one would dive down, catch a fish, and ride the wave. Another would move further ahead, watching the fish regroup, and then do the same thing. I took my shirt off, left my flip flops on the sand, and walked into the water.

    I know that waves have something to do with gravity and the moon. As I walked further into the sea, the sand dipped when the water reached my knees. But once past this line, the water rolled gently over my body, and I could feel myself floating. Fish swam around me as if I had been here since the island first rose out of the ocean. I could have stayed like this for hours.

'Hey.'

I turned around to see Lara. I raised my hand. Not drowning, but waving, as if I had seen somebody I used to know, but didn't know what to say. I went back to looking at life under the water. To the fish I was a refracted image. Lara came into the sea wearing the bikini she had worn on the first day on the island. She swam whilst trying to keep her hair dry. I smiled. She got closer.

'I didn't mean to hurt you.'

I shrugged.

'You can't protect stupid all the time.' It was a sort of Forest Gump way of saying I was just as much to blame for all this. 'I had a crazy idea I was going to get famous. But from now on, I'm just going to focus on my character and get the job done.'

And this was true. Now older, I know I could edit my memories to either make me look bad or good, but in that moment, I was in the ocean feeling lost. It was that awkward pause between two people who had once been close. I didn't know what else to say.

'Be careful where you stand,' I said.

Lara looked down at her feet.

'Why, is there a jellyfish?'

'No. I've just done a wee, and the current is going towards you.'

She moved around. 'Don't worry, I do one every time I have an early morning dip. Best piss of the day. I really hope they keep our scene in.'

'The one on the courtyard by the pond?'

'No, the one last night underneath the big screen. I don't think the audience moved once.'

'Apart from Dave Dolly Frip,' I said. 'He kept rubbing something in his pocket.'

'I think you should write a book about the making of this film. At least the laughs would be intentional.'

We spent the next twenty minutes joking about some of the things that had happened on the island. It was good to chat with someone who was on the same wavelength. Did it make any difference that she was now sleeping with a woman instead of a man? Well, I must admit, at that stage in my life, I had seen a lot of two women kissing in certain artistic magazines and videos, but I had never actually had a laugh and a joke with someone who I knew was a bisexual or a lesbian. That is not a criticism of anyone or anything. It was just that in 1996 I had never moved in the those circles, so to speak. I knew there were plenty of gay actors, but lesbians were still in the shadows for some reason. I suppose it took me a while to say "fuck it" who cares. And of course, thank God for the internet. Turns out there were thousands of sexy lesbians just waiting to come out of that virtual corset closet. They just needed a magic wand.

I decided to go tell Sal Klimer that I was nothing like him. I would rather give up acting than change who I really was. I would also tell him it wasn't me who got the birds to attack his trailer. I walked past the canteen and picked up a baguette. It was all part of my new health kick. As I got to the executive's campsite. Klimer was out of his trailer, standing near a man I thought I recognised. Klimer pointed at me.

'There he is. And he's got more bread. I told you it was him.'
Everyone turned, and I fucked off into the jungle.

Just like Lara, I disappeared quickly into the bush. I was sure I had seen the man before. Was it some sort of supernatural event that Kurtis had conjured up? Then I remembered. It was the copper from the police van.

Bastad looked around for me, but the jungle was my friend. The last few weeks had allowed me to become accustomed to the environment. I quickly found a safe place to hide and listened as Bastad tried to push his way through the big storks and plants. He called out my name.

'I know you are here, Wells. Thought you could get away with it, you little piece of excrement. Didn't expect me to come this far, did you?' Bastad stopped. There in the undergrowth he thought he saw my baguette. He crept forward, slowly reached out, and gave it a tug. The bush moved. Bastad got both hands on it.

'You might as well come quietly.' He gave a few more tugs. John Kurtis, dressed as a donkey creature, came through the bushes and fell on top of the police officer. It was only then that Bastad realised he was holding a large rubber penis. One of the hookers walked past.

'You English. You all go crazy on holiday.'

Bastad called into the jungle. 'This is your last chance Liam. I could send one fax and have your friend Custard sent to prison.'

At that point, I knew I had to help my mate, and so I entered the scene, stage left, ready to do what was right.

Forty-three

Bastad took me to the laboratory. He set up his own video camera. I had never been formally interviewed before, but I had seen enough cop shows to know that filming someone in a room filled with jars of animal parts was probably not quite kosher. After going backwards and forwards, with me telling him I had no idea what he was talking about, it was Bastad who was seemingly beginning to break.

'Tell me you were in the car, and we can make a deal.'
I shook my head.
'I have no idea what you are talking about.'
'Do you remember saying how much you wanted to join the police?'
'I'll admit that Every breath You Take isn't a bad song, but they're not really my cup of tea.'
Bastad clenched his fist. 'Just bloody confess.'

The man had all the charm and warmth of an angry rottweiler pissing up a frosty lamp post. Then it suddenly dawned on me that Bastad had no evidence. He must have travelled here because he was in deeper shit than me.

'I'm terribly sorry,' I said. 'But it sounds as if you are the one who is about to get twenty-four points on your licence, and a couple of thousand pounds in fines.'

Bastad had one more throw of the dice.

'I take it you do know who William Custard is? Maybe it doesn't matter. But when I stopped him, he had a pair of those dashboard dolls of Ike and Tina turner, or someone like that. And do you know what was inside? Some ecstasy pills. We turned his mums house over. Had to smash in her back doors. Better safe than sorry. There were a few items that we believe were not totally legit.' Bastad let out a little laugh. 'The custody sergeant wanted him charged with straightforward possession, but I soon made him come around. Your little friend is a major dealer.' Now the smiling stopped. 'I've got his car seized in a police compound.' He leaned closer. 'When I get back and search it properly, I am going to plant an awful lot of drugs in the boot, and some of them are going to have your fingerprints. You can take the risk and not believe me. But I've got a book at home hidden behind the fish tank with everyone I've ever stitched up, including other police officers. Putting two little shits like you in prison is going to as easy as blowing snot into a hanky. So, let's start again, shall we?'

For the first time in my life, I thought I was really in trouble. This was the dark night of my soul. But just when I thought I was out, Reginald Kincaid came in, clean shaven, wearing one of Grayson's expensive suits, an eye patch, and a briefcase.

'I am here to represent my client. Has he been arrested for anything?'

'No,' replied Bastad. 'But.'

'Then he is free to go.'

Bastad stood up. 'Are you his legal representative?'

Kincaid nodded. 'I have a criminal practice that takes up a lot of my time.'

'You're a Human Rights lawyer?'

This seemed to enrage Kincaid. 'How dare you. How fucking dare you. I've represented everyone from the Scopes trial to Kramer verses Kramer. What is my client accused of?'

I stood up.

'It's about some speeding tickets,' I said.

Kincaid gasped, unable to believe it.

'What? What fucker said that?' He turned to Bastad. 'Are you telling me the police can't catch burglars, but anyone going a few miles over the speed limit deserves to be fucking hounded to the ends of the earth?'

I could tell Bastad was not used to being spoken to in that manner; but Kincaid walked and talked like a barrister, and so he wasn't going to risk getting deeper into the shit.

'I wasn't even the driver,' I said. 'I wasn't even in the car.'

'What?' Cried Kincaid. He turned to Bastad. 'Are you some sort of buffoon who enjoys wasting taxpayers' money coming here?'

'No,' Bastad replied. 'I paid for this myself.'

'So, you admit you are a gormless chief superintendent.'

'Actually, I'm a gormless chief constable.' He looked closer. 'Haven't I seen you somewhere before?'

Kincaid helped me out of the operating theatre.

'Indubitably, as everyone on the island will tell you, I have spent many years at the bar.'

Bastad turned off his video camera.

'The boat comes back tomorrow. Once he's in England, he's all mine.'

'And I shall be reporting you to the RSPCA,' Kincaid replied. 'Playing Donkey Kong is a wonderfully innocent childhood game that is enjoyed everywhere in the world. But playing with a Donkey's dong is an offence even on this island. Good day to you sir. Good day.'

Once outside, my solicitor wanted to know all the facts.

'What happened?'

'We nicked the registration plate of a police van, stuck it to my mate's car, and got eight speeding tickets.'

Kincaid took out a carton of milk. Inside was a bottle of whiskey. 'You have absolutely no integrity. If you ever finish with acting, become a lawyer. You can't write your way out of this one, unless we can come up with a cunning plan.'

Forty-four

I was now hiding in the jungle, fighting for survival, relying only on my wits, living off spicy chicken burritos, Jamaican rum punch, and twelve grams of cannabis. It was tough twelve hours, but I made it. As 9am broke, I woke up and decided to forage for breakfast. It was slim pickings; just muesli, eggs, bacon, toast, croissants, pancakes, yoghurts, doughnuts, fruit medley, and coco pops. The crew was finishing up whatever was left in the kitchen; the hookers were getting in their last knockings before everyone left, and I had an idea.

The production schedule listed just a few more scenes to shoot, with me in most of them. The problem was I didn't know if I was going to make it to the end of the day, let alone the film. I had one more scene with Lara, which was going to be bittersweet in so many ways. But I also had to avoid Bastad, which was going to be difficult on such a small island. Some of the executives believed he was a member of BAFTA, and as such offered him access to every set. I knew that he was going to spend every waking hour hunting me down. I needed help on the ground. I found it in the heavens.

As I walked through the jungle, I heard a drum beating a slow rhythm and a woman chanting in a strange language. I found Kurtis sitting next to what I can only describe as a witch. She was kitala, one of the extras. Kurtis seemed to be in a trance. Kitala cast a set of runes onto the ground.

'Odin says there is a man who is trying to ruin your film.'
Kurtis stopped.

'Does he have a name?'
Kitala shook her head.

'He has many faces. But he will appear as a statue. He is the one you must stop.'

'Will I get my job back?' Kurtis asked her.
Kitala threw the runes again, looked at them, and shook her head. 'Odin only sees the shadows of the future. It is up to you to see the light and act upon it.'

I leant in and asked my own question.

'Can you ask Odin if I manage to finish the film without getting arrested?'
Kitala picked up the runes, shook them in her hand, cast a magical incantation, and then let them fall where they may. She looked at the ancient symbols.

'Fuck knows. He's now on a tea break.'
I gave her the last of my weed and decided to make my own future. As I headed toward costume and make-up, I knew the

only place to hide was in the middle of a crowd. There was only one woman who could help me.

'I need your help,' I said to Eve. 'The police want to take me away before the film finishes. I just need to do a couple more scenes.'

Eve put down a dress and looked at me.

'What do they want you for, fraud?'

I decided to explain what I had done by starting with the question: 'Have you ever had a speeding ticket?'

Within an hour I was dressed up as a type of mutant leopard. Eve used a spray gun to give me a faded yellow skin, then finished marking the black dots on my arms.

'So, you're not gay? But that night when we slept together in the same tent you didn't try to take advantage of me? Shame.'

Was she flirting? Even after all the crap, I was still a young man on holiday. And even though I wasn't quite sure if she was joking or not, I made a mental note to find out at some point.

Now was the time to test all my acting skills. I had to pretend to be an extra. I walked out of the hut and past a few executives, none of them seemed interested. For the final scenes a lot of the crew members were being dressed up as Borlocks or Wokners. They were told to be acting as if they were agitated. What made it easier was that the main island police had arrived. The executives thought they were looking for Kurtis, and so told them the man they were looking for might be dressed as a donkey and the extras might know something.

Unfortunately, upon seeing the police, the extras and the crew began to quickly move illegal substances and porn/drug paraphernalia into the jungle. When the police came across the various bongs and sex toys, they wondered what sort of film was being made here? As for me, the only safe hiding place would be in one of the hooker's tents. I chose the one with the cat. I paid my money, and made my way in. The smell was the closest I have ever been to a Hollywood production meeting. I looked around the tent.

'You have flooring,' I said. 'And a fan, and a shower. Is that a television with a built-in video player?'

The hooker patted the television.

'I like to watch Friends,' she said. You go under bed when I have any business. If I do anal I have my feet hanging off side.'

'It's half past ten in the morning,' I replied. 'The film crew don't put in that much effort when they're on overtime pay.' She shook her head. 'They English. Always come here on tea break. They don't do anything after lunch.'

And so, I spent a few uncomfortable hours under a squeaky camp bed, dressed as a leopard, being stared at by a cat, whilst my agent Artie Fufkin ball banged his baloney into the hooker while he sang.

'Hooray for Pollywood.'

At the same time, the hooker kept telling Artie, 'Go lower, go lower.'

Artie, his head jerking, didn't understand, and simply kept singing in a deeper voice as the bed creaked loudly until the climax. He certainly took ten percent of my pay that morning.

At lunchtime I joined a few of the extras in their costumes and noticed a split had developed in the camp. The biggest drunkards and druggies were dressed up as Borlocks. Those who were a bit more sensible were mutants in uniform. After weeks of being trapped on the island, some of the Wokners were taking their role more from the Stanford prison experiment than the script. Things were becoming a bit tense. I saw Cameron, standing proud between a pair of old Borlocks, and joined them. Everyone was speaking about the police being on the island. The real uniforms had caused a bit of a stir. I told them they were after me, not the contraband. Cameron said it was a shame, as the next scene was for everyone to start drinking the bottles of serum. What the Wokners didn't know was that the milk in the bottles had been replaced by a mixture of alcohol and cannabis. There was certainly a method to Cameron's madness.

By the evening most of the extras were drunk or stoned or both. I managed to get near to the white house and meet Eve. The spots came off easily, but the yellow stayed on. It didn't matter, this was a black and white film. She handed me my cabin boy shirt and trousers, and the cutlass I had when I first landed. I didn't have time to take off my tail, so I wrapped it around my waist and stuffed it down the front of my trousers, making it look as if I had a baton a Jamaican sprinter would be proud of. Ironically, the only way I was going to get through the next scene without being caught was to speed through it. Lara, dressed as Lola the panther woman, saw me just before we went into the courtyard.

'The police are after you.'

'I know.' That was my Han Solo moment. I kissed her on the cheek. 'Whatever happens, stay in character.'
She was about to thank me and then looked down at my trousers.

'Are you excited about the possibility of winning an Oscar?'

'You can be blasé about some things Lara,' I said, 'But not this film. It's going to be a disaster of Titanic proportions, and we're going to go down with it.'

The runner came over.

'Ready to go?'
This was it. Ride or die. 'And…action.'

Forty-five

Lara sat by the fishpond, looking at the Charlie Chaplin figurine. I ran in carrying my cutlass. She gasped.
Lara: 'How did you get such a magnificent weapon?'
Me: 'From my father's side of the family. My nan always told me I came from a long line of sea men.' I put the sword down. 'Lola. We must leave the camp tonight before they burn the village huts down. I know you don't like being on the water or any sort of boat, but I want you to come on my big one.'
Lola looked down at the bulge in my trousers, before returning to my face.

'Could you ever love a giant pussy?'
I grabbed hold of her. 'It's going to be hard. People will be watching, and it could get messy at the end. Are you ready to take that risk?' I placed one leg on the side of the pond. My thick sausage like tail had moved halfway down my inner thigh. 'I want to take you to a magical place where we can be free to make mad passionate love in the moonlight.'
Lara: 'Where?'
Me: 'Droitwich. Once you get over the smell from the sewage works its wonderful.'

From the bars on the window, we hear the roar and clapping of the creatures.

Lara: 'What about Dr Farquar?'

Me: 'Quickly. You must decide before they blow the dong of Diabolos and come on our faces. I mean, come on. Our faces are not welcome here anymore. Dr Farquar wanted you to make love to me just so he could have a new generation of servile Wokners to use as propaganda. He doesn't care what gender, race, or even species they are; as long as they are all ready to shout down anyone who disagrees, force out those whose opinion they think doesn't matter, and banish all the non-believers.'

#

The Wokners came into the courtyard. I held up my sword. We got on our marks ready for the fight scene. At this point one of the island police officers walked into the set. We all stopped. The police officer looked at the camera, then at me, then at the Wokner, then at my trousers.

'Is that gun in your pocket?'

Jane Dough was about to come on set, when the police officer took out his gun. Shit just got real.

'You were speeding,' the police officer said to me.

'Yes,' said the Wokner from under his mask. 'I did think his character was saying his lines rather quickly; but if we remember Lawrence Olivier and his portrayal of Hamlet.'
I pushed the Wokner into the pond.

'Oh, bugger,' he called out. 'Gordon, I'm going down.'
Lola pushed the policeman into the pond. It wasn't quite the fight the director was expecting.

'Keep going,' said Jane. 'We can edit this later.'

Diddler then came into the courtyard on a mobility scooter. I turned and pointed the sword at him. Diddler growled at me.

'Some Bastad is after you.'
Another Wokner came onto the set, dressed as a gorilla in uniform.

'He prefers to be called Dr Farquar. My God, what's happened to Gerald?' He tried to help the first Wokner out of the water.

I could see some of the executives coming towards the set, and the other police officer trying to open the door. Bastad appeared and looked through the iron bars. If he had any brains he could have just walked around and caught me. The second Wokner stood by the edge of the pond calling out to Gerald. Diddler tried to do a three point turn in the mobility scooter. I knew my big speech was going to be cut short somewhat. The first Wokner screamed.

'Look out Gordon.'

I kicked the second Wokner into the water and then shouted at Diddler.

'Times up, Davros.'

I pressed down on the pedal, and Diddler also went into the pond. Then I kissed Lola, just for shits and giggles, and waved at Cameron, who had got Dave Dolly Grip to rig the camera crane. The winch came down. I grabbed it, and was lifted out as more Wokners, the executives, Bastad, and the second police officer barged in.

Jane Dough looked around at the chaos, completely unfazed.

'Shut the clapper, get the toy goldfish out of the fake gorilla's arse, and let's get ready to roll again.'

#

I ran through the darkness of the jungle back to the Borlock's village. The executives had long since stopped coming down here. Knowing that the film was going to be wrapped up very soon, the place had become the twenty-first birthday party for Sodom and Gomorrah. The Borlocks, made up of Australian,

South African, and British beach bums, all knew that their time was nearly up. This was an island, miles away from civilisation, and they were all wearing masks. They continued to smoke their joints and showed no fear. Bastad arrived next.

'I'm looking for a man.'

'For buggery?' one of the Borlock's called back.

'No. He's more of a boy, actually.'

Tango, sporting a large orange afro, stepped forward.

'Pervert.'

Bastad looked around. 'He is unlawfully at large.'

'Receiver,' said the campest creature in the camp. 'Are you a friend of Gordon's?'

'His name is Liam Wells. He is to be taken back to England to face prosecution.'

'For what?'

Bastad knew he couldn't lie.

'....Some speeding tickets. It's a statute law.'

The donkey creature stepped forward, placed its hands on its hips, and let its enormous phallus swing gently in the breeze.

'Nobody leaves the island until filming finishes tomorrow. That is the law of the island.'

'Are you a Scottish donkey?' Bastad asked.

'It's better than being an English twat,' said Kurtis from under the mask. 'Go away now.'

Bastad walked away, but decided to find out who the donkey was, and have him arrested as well.

Forty-six

Everyone was ready. Geno Wright and Grayson Cunlick waited in the actor's camp. I hid in Dame Helen's tent, as I figured even a chief inspector wasn't going to start rooting through the drawers of respectability. Some of the film crew were dressed as Russian soldiers. This seemed to comprise of wearing a large bear hat with the hammer and sickle on it. They were hanging communist flags and pictures of Stalin. In the original script the communist army were going to collect a few mutants and take them back to Moscow. Arlen Parker was meant to defeat them, but things had gone pear shaped since the start of filming. Even the production team didn't really know what was going on anymore. But they had flown over the tents, uniforms, and flags. They were sticking to the schedule even if everyone including me had given up. In defiance, the prop unit had changed some of the pictures of Stalin into Klimer. I stuck my head out of Dame Helen's flaps when I heard Jane Dough speaking.

'I've got some bad news,' she said. 'I have just been informed by one of the executives that Sal Klimer has control of the final cut for this film. It's in his contract to decide how this picture turns out, and it's going to cost too much for the studio to buy it back and for me to edit it. Sal is being such an arse gravy, that if I was to make a film about the life of Sal Klimer, I wouldn't have Sal Klimer in it.' She didn't have to look at me to say what was coming next. 'And it probably means some of you may not even make it into the theatrical release.'

I doubt if the guy would piss on me if I was on fire. I stepped forward.

'Sal doesn't like me. And the reason the police are here is because I got a few speeding tickets. Chief inspector Bastad wants to put me in prison system. I'm willing to hand myself in and go back home right now if it helps you finish the film.'

Dame Helen stood up.

'No. We are a team, and you're staying. What can Sal do with an unfinished film, wipe it like a bad shit?'

Jane shook her head.

'Only Klimer and Farlow have been paid up front. All of us, including the crew, are on a contract to complete the production. If we don't finish this, none of us will get paid. It's going to be a long night until everything is wrapped, and if we are not on that boat in the morning, we will have to make our own way home. The best thing we can do is go out the way we always planned. With a bang.'

Everyone agreed; but there was still one issue to be resolved.

'Geno should be the love interest with Lara,' I said. 'There is no point filming the escape scene twice, especially if I get caught by the fuzz.' I don't think Jane was sure what that word meant, and she scratched her crutch.

'You know that means you're out of the picture,' said Jane. 'You might not even get a named credit. These next scenes can only be done once, and we can never go back again.'
I nodded. In some ways those lines were the best piece of advice I ever had. Now that the issue of who was going to be the lead had been resolved, people began to get ready for a film shoot that would last well into the night.

Kincaid placed all the bottles on the bar.

'We have come to our journey's end, dear boy. Everything must go, including my box of delights.' He lifted the lid. Inside were pungent joints and a selection of pleasure pills. As people went into their tent to pack. Lara came up to me.

'Thanks.'

'What for?' I asked.

'This could be my only chance of getting to Hollywood. For every ten male actors in a film there is one woman; and she is usually all teeth and tits. Luckily, they are my best features. I think you changed your part to save me.'
She was probably right. I had been bought up to be a gentleman. If they ever made a film about the Titanic, I would

be one of those men who would have let women and children onto the lifeboats first.

'If I was you, I would look at getting another part before this film comes out. I think this is going to bomb.' I was hoping she wouldn't be shocked. She wasn't.

'I know,' she replied. 'But the bosses back in Hollywood are still going to watch it to see just how crap it is. Hopefully they will give me another chance. It's you I feel sorry for.'

At that moment I was more worried about Bastad catching me. The two main island police officers had left to get a bigger boat and would be returning tomorrow. If Bastad found me before then, he would make sure I wouldn't be able to escape. I went down to the film crews camp and told Cameron and the cooks why the police were after me. They were not pleased. So, they conducted their own little show.

In celebration of the last full day of filming (and Farlow managing to stay alive), the executives had arranged for themselves a farewell meal. It consisted of chowder for starters. Among the cook's secret blend of herbs and spices was a soupçon of ecstasy. The main course was a selection of lobsters and speciality sausages. A sort of surf and girth. All the sauces had been liberally doused with cocaine. In fact, there was so much left on the island, it was put into the salt and pepper shakers and sprinkled over the fries. The desert was a choice of chocolate fudge brownie. Of which there was so much cannabis in it, I was sure the Hollywood executives would smell it; but they were already so high on their own success they didn't notice anything was wrong. The other option was Peanut Brittle. Or as the cook kept calling it "Peanus Brittle" I was pretty sure she had put something in this one, but I really didn't want to know. To be fair, most people in Hollywood are so far removed from reality, being off their heads was not going to come as a major shock.

My only real worry was Brandon Farlow. He had already eaten two Pot Noodles before he arrived for the meal; and those things have got more chemicals in them than a night cap from Bill Cosby. He sat and put those foot-long brown wieners in his mouth quicker than the Kardashian family at a basketball team training camp. Luckily, the amount of chocolate fudge hash brownie he put away would balance out any cocaine high. I later heard that he left a load in his toilet so big, dark, and sticky, the cleaners thought a bear had wandered into his trailer and taken a shit. It was an honour to work with such an old pro.

The Hollywood executives finished off the meal with bottles of champagne cocktails, made by our convivial host Reginald Kincaid. God knows what he spiked everyone with. But do you want to know the best thing out of all this? Among these chumps celebrating their power was Jerry Bastad. Some still thought he was a member of BAFTA and had invited him. It was a real joy to watch as he ate and drank every course. It would mean he would barely be able to wipe his own arse in a few hours' time, and as far as I was concerned, it meant "The kid stays in the picture, and on the island."

Forty-seven

Down in the village, Diddler stood on a box grabbing his Borlocks as they stole more bottles of serum and drunk them.

Diddler: 'Just one. Just one.'

But the Borlocks did not seem to care. They were waving and dancing around the communist flag while the others clapped. Even some of the Wokners had joined in.

Diddler: 'You can only have a revolution?' Diddler lashed out with the whip. 'If the white house say so.' He struck again. 'If you don't eat your meat, you can't have any pudding.'

He flicked it out again. Tango caught the end of it and did not let go. Everyone stopped. Diddler pulled on the whip handle, Tango pulled back. Diddler pulled harder; Tango pulled then end, then let go, sending Diddler flying backwards *off the box. Tango clapped out his orders. Without a word, some of the creatures flicked the sticky substance all over Diddler's face and clothes.*

Diddler: *'Stop. Only Dr Farquar is allowed to do that to me.'* He got up and pushed the creatures away.

Tango: 'It magic juice.'

Diddler: 'You have a voice?' '

Tango: 'We know now that you have been trying to fool us all along. There was no virus, and you did not have the cure. You didn't want to help us, you just wanted to stay in power.'

Diddler quickly grabbed the Horn of Diabolos and blew into the conch. The high-pitched parp had the Pavlovian effect of causing his Borlocks to drop, enabling him to drive away in the mobility scooter. But this time some of the Borlocks decided to follow.

Near the white house, myself and Kincaid carried torches and went to find the others. We were stopped by a Wokner, who decided not to get too close when I waved the flaming torch. This one looked strangely familiar. Although its face was that of a jackal, I noticed it had tattoos of Swallows on each hand.

Me: 'Captain look. They're the same tattoos of small birds that Kenneth the ships stoker had, before he disappeared.'

The Wokner growled.

Kincaid: 'It looks more like Bernard the chef who had the tattoo of a guitar on his back.'

Me: 'No captain. I used to listen to the men talking at night. It was always Benny plucks and Kenny swallows. Kenny has another tattoo of a dragon on his arm.' I moved the torch. The Wokner raised his arm. A Chinese dragoon stared back at us.

The uniformed creature growled and pushed us away.

Kincaid: 'Kenny. If you can still hear us, where is lady Ruffsnatch?'

The creature stepped aside and pointed towards the laboratory.

 Meanwhile, in the jungle, Diddler stopped the mobility scooter when he saw Klimer step into the road.

Klimer: 'Have you seen my friend Lawton?'

Diddler. 'I think he was dragged away by the Borlocks.'

Klimer (shakes head): 'The poor bastard.'

Diddler drove away in the mobility scooter as the sound of clapping grew louder.

 Klimer stood in the middle of the path, deep in the heart of the jungle, as the Borlock's came towards him.

Klimer: My name is Arlen Parker. 'I'm an American, and I am here to save all of you.' He then shot the nearest one. Before he could save anymore by killing them, the Borlocks picked him up and carried him away.

Klimer: 'If you just let me bomb the whole village, all of you will have been liberated.'

Inside the white house, Dame Helen was at the dining room table, tied to a chair.

Kincaid: 'Lady Ruffsnatch. He's not serving his overcooked tuna pasta bake again, is he?'

Dame Helen (shakes head): 'Worse. Shepherd's pie. I came here to collect Grayson, but Dr Farquar wants him to be part of his communist utopia. I'm all for socialism, as long as I don't have to pay for it. Farquar told me I wasn't rich or famous enough to be able to get away with such hypocrisy. All the body swapping laws, racial theories, and rewriting history, is just an illusion to keep everyone divided whilst he and his cohorts stay at the top.'

Kincaid: 'Where is he now?'

Dame Helen: 'The white house. I think they are going to get my son to make love to Lola.'

Kincaid coughed slightly and glanced at me.

Kincaid: 'The same son who has seen Mamma Mia fourteen times?'

Dame Helen: 'What do you think they are going to do in that room, captain?'

The old man took out his cigar and thought about it.

Kincaid: 'I can remember watching this Dutch film once. A woman had gone to a health farm, and this big lad had just escaped from prison. And this woman says -'

Dame Helen (looking at my sword): 'I hope you know how to use that weapon.'

Kincaid: 'You've seen the film as well?'

Dame Helen (picking up a silver carving knife): 'I thought the acting was mediocre, and the ending was a bit sloppy. Well, once more into the breach, dear friends.'

We headed off towards the laboratory.

Forty-eight

Sal Klimer had originally demanded the white house set piece to be the highlight of the film. It would have taken something that looked like a low budget psychological horror and turned it into a high explosive action thriller. It was what the executives called, "The trailer shot". The script may have changed since production started. The character of Arlen Parker was not the same; but Sal Klimer still wanted to go out with a Dirty Dozen ending. It probably would have helped if he had not had a six of slices of the chocolate fudge brownie that evening.

Klimer had his shirt strategically ripped as he was laid down and tied to the cross by the Borlock's. Why a large wooden cross? This was what Sal Klimer wanted. The Last Temptation was nominated for a couple of Oscars, so this should do the same. Klimer also knew that this was the only way he could get one up on the old fart Brandon Farlow.

As the extras carried the cross towards the hill, some of the Borlocks' sighed "fucking hell" under their breath as if they were stuck in a Beatles song. This could have been a short take. The creatures tying a man to a cross. Then cut to the hill, and the cross being raised upright. But Klimer made them carry him for the half mile through the jungle, and then halfway up the hill. The scene probably would have been quite moving, if the extra in the donkey costume didn't keep shouting in a Scottish accent 'drop the cunt.'

As well as Parker looking wasted, his once magnificent moustache, having been recently sniffing a hooker's sweaty ring piece, was now losing its lustre. As Parker was erected towards the heavens, one half of his moustache dropped down.

#

As we headed towards the laboratory, a glow came from the valley. The Borlocks huts were burning. It would give Klimer's crucifixion just the right level of pathos and lighting. We met Geno. He had been down to the beach and seen the communist camp. We needed to get off the island tonight.

The Borlocks were now clapping and calling to the Wokners to remember who they really were. Beyond the white house, the Wokners were calling back. They let all the caged animals escape from the zoo, offering the gorillas bottles of serum. It would appear the fake virus that the white house had produced just to give the mutants something to fear, was now turning into a worry for those at the top. We could hear clapping in the distance. The Borlocks were almost in our faces. Things were certainly getting hairy.

Inside the laboratory, there were surgical instruments, bubbling glass vats, and bolts of electricity. Lara was lying star shaped on the operating table, her ankles and wrists were tied with leather bands. The silky smoothness of her inner thighs glowed under the shining lights. A sheer white dress barely covered her taut stomach, and the gentle heaving of her young supple breasts caused her nipples to twitch like a rabbit's nose (Dave Dolly Grip had been married for over twenty years, so he had got the camera as close as he could). Brandon Farlow, dressed in a white doctor's coat and pith helmet held up a pumpkin. Brandon: 'No more inequality, no more history, no more sexuality, no more humanity. Begin the orgasmatron.'

One of the Wokners pressed a button, and the lights above the operating table began to glow. Grayson appeared in a black leather catsuit. He took a sniff of something from a small bottle. The music grew louder. The dancing got faster. Grayson walked towards Lara and held up a turkey baster. The Wokners roared as Geno ran forward, punched Grayson, and began to unit Lara.

Geno (to Brandon): 'You crazy, Farquar.'

Brandon: 'Crazy. People who have worked hard all their lives, paid taxes, stayed out of trouble, never complained, never protested; only to realise they are no better than animals on a farm. My creatures are the future. A fool who knows how to press buttons will be twice as productive as a clever man in the wrong job.'

Geno: 'And what happens when they disagree with your politics?'

Brandon: 'How are things working out for you back in America?' (That line wasn't in the script; and whether it was 1936, or 1996, it was still a powerful comment. Both Farlow and Wright stayed in character).

Geno: 'You don't get to choose how and what I should think. You are not a God.'

The crowd outside was getting noisier.

Brandon (laughing): 'The only way you can stop a wild creature from attacking is to kill it. But your modern morality has made you weak. You don't want equality, you want happy slaves hidden away in the darkness, while you look for a new God to follow.' He threw then pumpkin and went to the back door.

Some of the Wokners by the window shrieked. Brandon looked out to see the Borlock's village in flames, and the silhouette of Klimer on the cross. What should have been Klimer's big speech about justice and democracy was ruined because he was too stoned to speak. Instead, he sang 'Always look on the bright side of life,' while slowly urinating in his trousers. This was never going to put out the fire that was surrounding him. Back in the Laboratory, Brandon turned to us.

Brandon: 'Arlen Parker's been hung up by the Borlock's.'
Kincaid: 'The poor bastard. I think I would rather be crucified.'

Geno took my sword and cut Lara free. Grayson tried to pull them back. I took the turkey baster and fired half a pint of monkey jizz into Grayson's face.

Dame Helen: 'The horror, the horror.'

We ran out of the laboratory just as the Borlocks arrived and smashed down the back door. They fought with the Wokners still loyal to Brandon.

Brandon: 'My word is the law. No other thoughts are allowed.'

A large orangutang stepped forward.

Tango: 'Then you must be silenced.'

The creatures clapped and shrieked as Brandon was dragged to the operating table. Some of them groaned. He was still a big old unit and was now so stoned that he kept eating in-between his lines. A gorilla mask was put on his face. Diddler was brought in. The Borlocks put a monkey mask on his face. Tango: 'Lube them up, and then put them to the gorilla cage.'

As the mutants cheered, two of the Wokners realised that the other humans had escaped.

We ran towards the courtyard, which was already burning. Lara led us to a secret door as the white house started to collapse. Kincaid and I were last to go through. As I ran past the pond, I saw my little porcelain figure of Charlie Chaplin. I went to get it, but Kincaid grabbed hold of me.

Kincaid: 'Forget it, Jack; it's a china clown.'

We ran through the jungle. Kincaid as Captain Rimlick, with his new eye, could now see better in the dark than any of us. In the distance we could hear the creatures clapping as they destroyed the white house. They knew we were heading towards the pier. I stopped to help Dame Helen as she struggled to keep up. Grayson turned.

Grayson: 'Mother, I'm going back.'

Dame Helen: 'Are you mad? You are a Ruffsnatch.'

Grayson: 'I don't need family when I have my own followers.'

Dame Helen: 'All I have ever done is try to raise you to be a decent human being. But because I have different opinions to you, I am somehow always wrong. The only thing I wish I had done back home was tell you to take more responsibility for your actions rather than demanding instant gratification. If you want to stay on your own little island, I will not stop you. But let me give you one final piece of wisdom. It's easy to surround yourself with people who will always tell you what you want to hear; but that doesn't mean it always be the truth.'

It was too late. Grayson had already run back into the darkness.

As we moved down to the beach, I saw a light, and I walked towards it.

A hand reached out and pulled me to the ground.

#

'Gotcha.' The light from a video camera revealed chief inspector Bastad's face.

Now, this image may have carried more dramatic impact if the police officer didn't have a large ring of chocolate fudge brownie smeared around his mouth.

'No more running away, you little piece of shit.' He smiled (chunks of chocolate between his teeth). 'I'm going to make sure you suffer. I'm going to punish you until you even start confessing to things you haven't done.'

'Please,' I tried to explain. 'I've done nothing wrong.' Bastad tried to pick up his camera. 'Do you know how many innocent men I've charged? I've stitched up loads; and I've got no problem doing the same to you.'
As I looked around, I came across a tin filled with grey paint. 'But there are two main issues here,' I said. 'The first is, we are in the middle of a jungle.'
Bastad waited. 'What's the second?'
I stood up. 'You're a cunt. I covered him in grey paint then ran off into the all-encompassing darkness of the jungle.

Bastad flicked the dripping paint from his hands and took a deep breath. He brushed it away from his eyes.

'Where have you gone, you lousy little piece of-'
I appeared from nowhere and hit him in the face with the paint tin. Then I ran back into the jungle. I could hear him coming after me.

We raced over tree roots and brushed passed palm leaves. Finally, the drugs caught up with Bastad, literally. Cameron, dressed as a monkey, was clearing out the bottom of the cannabis barrel for one last hit on the shell bong. As he concentrated all his efforts on another smoke, the barrel rolled down the slope, gaining speed, until it hit Bastad, taking him clean out. Cameron found him, half unconscious, covered in grey paint. Being a young man in the film industry, Cameron did the decent thing. He helped Bastad crawl into the barrel, then rolled it down towards the beach.

#

I joined the others. We reached the beach and saw the ship at the end of the jetty. The tide was at its highest point. Soon it would be too late to get over the barrier reef. We could also see Geno and Lara running towards us. They had drawn the mutants away from us to give us a chance; but the Wokners and the Borlocks were getting closer. The gates to the jetty were locked. I tried, but they would not open. Reginald Kincaid, wearing his captain's hat, rushed forwards and headbutted the gates. They busted open.

We ran. I climbed up into the ship and moved the anchor. As I lifted Dame Helen, in full Victorian Lady Ruffsnatch regalia (a real trooper), I saw the mutants stop at the gates, apart from a female fox creature. As it went for Geno, Lara jumped on her, and they fought. Kincaid started the engine.

Me: 'We must leave, captain.'

Kincaid (watching two busty women fight): 'Just five more minutes of foxy boxing.'
Me: 'There's no time.'

Lara and the fox were now tearing into each other. More Mutants arrived on the beach. The Wokners, less afraid of fire than the Borlocks, carried burning torches. Eventually, Lola killed the lady fox, but she was mortally wounded. She smiled at Geno, then died. The creatures began to move closer. The ship was moving away from the jetty. I threw a rope down.
Me: 'Mr Lawton.'
Geno dived into the water, swam out, caught the rope and climbed up. We then watched as the creatures clapped and howled while in the distance the white house burned.

#

Chief inspector Bastad crawled out of the drugs barrel. He turned the barrel upside down and stood on it. From the boat he looked like a statue, his head covered with cannabis dust. The script just said that the mutants fight amongst themselves as if they had become beasts again. Most of them were so wasted they were slapping the air and dancing. The Hollywood executives had taken off most of their suits and were wandering around, laughing at shells. Bastad held out his warrant card and demanded they all leave the nightclub and go home to bed. I saw him fall. And then I saw the donkey creature stop and squat over his open mouth. And then it happened.

'Arrivederci, ya bastad.'

We waited as the lighting rigs were moved and the camera crews filmed the fires and the creatures watching our ship leave the island. It was meant to signify that no man is an island. The ending was spoiled somewhat when Jane Dough picked up the megaphone.

'Why the fuck is there a mad sex donkey and a stoned policeman on the beach?'

Forty-nine

As we sailed into the moonlight, Dame Helen gave her prophetic speech about the folly of man when he desires to be a God. That you cannot try and take over a native culture and force a society to agree on everything, whether it was an idea, a viewpoint, or just a feeling. There are some things that you can never change. It was the sort of speech that the old actors loved to give. Behind us you could see the white house in flames. Those mutants left on the beach would now have to start making their own decisions. Although her part had been small, Dame Helen had shone.

Those who know the original novel are aware that at that moment we didn't know if Lara's sacrifice had been in vain. Was she still alive? On paper, it held a certain composition; was this really the end. Could she even be pregnant, and so set the ball rolling for when a new band of travellers arrive? Speaking of balls, at least the film left the question of whether Dr Farquar and Diddler were alive or dead up to the audience.

Instead, the cinematic end was a different shot. Our ship sailed away into the mist. There was a close up as the camera moved onto the captain's deck (I said deck). Now able to look out to sea and sail himself, Kincaid looked out at the darkness. A close up of his face. Where his eye patch used to be, the rectangular pupil of a goat's eye turned slightly, reminding us that there was one person who had been operated on that had escaped from the island. He took off his cap to reveal two small horns now growing on the top of his head and bleated out a small "Baaah."

#

And that was it. We couldn't reshoot any of the scenes, as the white house had really been burnt down. As the sun rose the film crews were still damping down the fires. Others were packing away equipment into storage cases. Now daylight, the Hollywood executives, who had been up all night, had turned into bestial idiots, splashing about in the sea, their suits left on the beach, covered in crabs.

Reginald Kincaid and I stayed in costume and said goodbye to everyone by making them a farewell drink. Every hug and kiss was like a family member leaving with the promise to meet again soon. There was a new Bond film in the works, this one about a British warship that sinks in Chinese waters. There was another boat film, this one about the Titanic. There were a few films coming up about wizards, which always relied on an old English actor to play the part.

Kincaid certainly had a few choice words when the helicopters turned up again.

I heard that Artie Fufkin gave Sal Klimer the invoice for his stay on the island. Just under a million pounds. Klimer looked at all twenty-four pages of items it claimed he had bought in the last few weeks.

'What the fuck is this, Hitler's gas bill?'

'No sir. Your contract had the proviso that you would pay for your own food and beverages.'

'I was drinking my own urine before I even got here.' Klimer went through the pages. 'Look at all this. Two hundred bottles of tequila, three hundred bottles of rum, a hundred bottles of vodka, and four hundred bottles of gin. Not to mention the crates of red and white wine, two thousand crates of beer, champagne, slimline tonic; and what the fuck is eight crates of Pot Noodle. Drugs? You want the world to think I'm smoking Chinese Cannabis, Artie?

'Mr Klimer,' said Artie Fufkin, Pollywood Productions. 'Your signature is on the invoice.'

The invoice was the piece of paper Kincaid had got Klimer to sign.

I later found out that Klimer had the signature checked by experts, and was told it was his. Whether this had any outcome on the way the film was cut I don't know. I was still keeping an eye out for Chief Inspector Bastad. The space cake he had eaten last night was powerful enough to knock out Woody Harrelson, so it was some heavy shit. When he woke up on the beach covered in paint and seaweed, he knew there had been something in his mouth, but was not sure what. He stood up and watched the police boat arrive. The police looked at the half naked executives tripping in the sea, a human corn on the cob demanding everyone be arrested, and mutants having sex with each other; and decided to go visit the cooks.

I packed up what was in my tent and took one last walk to the beach. I had decided to give myself up. Lara walked over to me.

'I guess this is the end?'

'For me it is,' I said. 'I bet I don't even get two lines when its released.'

We walked down the beach until our feet were in the sea.

'Loaded magazine have booked me for a bikini shoot…and a couple of pictures of me dressed as a sexy cat.'

I wished her good luck and told her she would be OK. I was going to say something about how we had some good times, but it sounded a bit phoney in my head.

'I'm sorry for treating you like crap.'

'I agree,' she replied. 'But you did make me laugh.' She kissed me on the cheek and headed back to the camp.

I looked to see Grayson and Kincaid coming towards me. We all watched Lara as she walked away. Grayson shook his head.

'I never believed that a man could be so bad in bed he could actually turn a woman into a lesbian, and then I met you.'

'It was a struggle,' I replied. 'But I got there in the end.'

'Speaking of which, how are you getting home?'
I looked at Grayson. 'By police escort, I think?'

'How about this?' Grayson rubbed his hands. 'You and Reggie help me take the boat back to Sydney harbour, then we catch a different flight? I've got "The Spy Who Loved Me" set up on deck. And I also believe that Reg has another video that may be of interest?'

From behind his back, Kincaid produced Bastad's video camera.

'Cameron gave it to me. It has the chief inspector threating to send you to prison unless you confess.' He smiled. 'Cameron also managed to film footage of what happened to the poor police officer and a donkey's appendage. I believe the phrase is called "Taking one for the team."'
We headed towards the pier.

By the time Bastad and the mainland police went down to the actors camp the place was empty. Just a few communists' flags in the sand. A note had been pinned to the bar:

Dear Bastad,

Our journey ends, not with a bang but with a rewind.

I have your video camera. Please cancel any warrants for my arrest and

release my friend Billy Custard.

I shall see you outside court on the 12th.

Up yours truly,

Liam Wells.

As he ripped it up, a squadron of helicopters flew overhead, blowing sand into his face. Me, I was already miles away, laughing as I sat on the deck wearing green moccasins, listening to Grayson and Kincaid talk about some of the cock ups they've had in the film business. In the wheel cabin we had placed the slightly burnt Charlie Chaplin figurine by the windscreen to guide us home.

Fifty

Dream it while you can.
 Oasis, Fade Away.

And so, the island we had colonised and laid waste in a matter of weeks, slowly watched us fade away. The police had to protect Sal Klimer as he was escorted to the helicopter, as so many people had threatened to hit him. From up in the air, he watched as another helicopter tried to lift his beautiful vintage trailer. Unfortunately, someone had unbolted every single nut and screw, and the tin can collapsed in a heap. The last thing Klimer saw was Artie Fufkin of Pollywood productions nodding his head towards Brandon Farlow. For once, he was right.

Farlow was luckier. He had survived the film. A real doctor was brought over to see if he was fit to fly, and it turned out he wasn't. He was sent to another island and forced to lose four stone before he could go back to America. He never did any chat shows to promote the film. Diddler was last seen running through the jungle, being chased by a sex starved monkey.

I heard the plane journey back was uneventful. A lot of the film crew hadn't slept for nearly two days. There were so many drugs floating around in their bodies that if the plane crashed into the sea the sharks would be stoned for weeks. There was talk of a new Owlman film possibly being made in London. Every member of the film crew said they wouldn't do it. They were more worried about a rumour of asbestos being found in the old film stages at Borehamwood, and a supermarket wanting to buy the land. Cameron reckoned that a film company should just buy the empty helicopter factory in Leavesden, but no one was listening.

Chief Inspector Bastad found the paint would not come off. He went between the final stragglers looking for me. Nobody knew where I had gone. The cook with the cat gave him the last of the chocolate fudge brownie; and as a special treat, she also gave him the clap.

When he arrived at Casablanca, the sniffer dogs nearly attacked him due to the amount of cannabis in his hair. The men in Customs and Excise got an old blind man to probe his anus. I was to find out later that Bastad was hated by the police so much that they kept him in the cells for three days, making him shit into a box like a cat just in case he had swallowed something nasty. I suppose both of us knew we were going to meet again at some point, and neither of us were expecting that this was the beginning of a beautiful friendship.

As soon as Dame Helen got home, she was offered a part on some film about Shakespeare. She said to me that it didn't matter how much time you were on screen for, its what you did with every frame that was important.

Fifty-one

A few weeks later, I was back in England ready for the big day. I got a new black suit, haircut, and new shoes (but no tie). A couple of photographers were waiting outside the building. I half hoped they would recognise me. I waited with a few others until my friend Billy Custard turned up (late). He was also wearing a suit. The security guards let him through. Then I waved at the crowd, and went in. I noticed the CCTV cameras. Big Brother had arrived later than expected. An usher asked me my name.

'Liam Wells.'

'Any relation to the author?' She asked.

'No.'

She checked her clipboard. 'Your in court number four.'

Chief Inspector Bastad was already there. His uniform had been freshly ironed. I couldn't tell where the creases stopped, and the man began. He had a smile on his face like a dead halibut.

'Welcome to my world,' he said. 'I promise to tell the judge not to go too hard on you.'

He seemed very sure of himself. If me and Billy got convicted, all the charges against Bastad would be dropped.

He would be free to continue his rise up the ranks, causing more pain and heartache, and that was just to other officers. We could be facing possible prison sentences. But if there was one thing I had learned on the island, it was that sentences, like the words on a page, can be changed. I shook my head.

'I think we are going to do this scene the way I want it to go.' I held up a pack of photographs. 'These are quite interesting. They work like the old "What the butler saw" machines you used to get on the pier. Each photograph is slightly different to the next; so, when you flick through them, it looks like everyone is moving.' I handed over the cards to Bastad.

He let them flip off his thumb. They started on the beach of Paradise Island, just near the pier. You saw Bastad fall, then turn over and lie on his back as the creatures fight around him. Kurtis, the donkey man, brayed at the moon, then crouched over Bastads face, letting that magnificent bulbous veiny penis slobber on the coppers nose. I can only say that what you saw next would be barred in fifty-nine countries. Luckily, Billy Custard was happy to speak.

'Those are professional quality pictures,' he said. 'It looks like you're covered in paint and cannabis. And then that's you gulping down a big smelly donkey dick. Talk about having the munchies.'

'I will say it's not real,' said Bastad. 'It doesn't prove anything.'

I took out a piece of paper.

'You are right. Film can be edited to show whatever the director wants. But a record of taped interview is very difficult to fake. I've watched the film, and made a few notes. I like the bit about a book at home behind the fish tank with everyone you've ever stitched up, including other police officers.'

Bastad snatched the paper from me. 'I am also arresting you for theft of a video camera.'

'I merely borrowed it,' I told him. 'Just to make copies of the cassette inside. That's why Billy here was late. He was dropping one off at police HQ to your chief inspector. I bet he's rushing round your house right now with a warrant. You might beat him if you leave now.

Bastad turned pink with rage. 'You are the most devious little shit I have ever come across. You have no morals whatsoever, you are willing to persecute others to get what you want, and you show all the signs of being sexual degenerate. Are you sure you don't want to join the police?'

I shook my head. I didn't want to spend my life dressing up and pretending to be someone I wasn't.

Bastad abandoned ship and ran out of court just as Reginald Kincaid arrived.

'Hurrah.'

He popped a bottle of champagne and handed out the plastic cups. It was a small victory, but in the big scheme of things, an important one, and everyone deserves the credits.

Postscript

But I was so much older then, I'm younger than that now. The film was an absolute mess. Sal Klimer demanded it to be re-edited show him in most scenes, giving the film no narrative whatsoever. The critics said that the only thing worthy of an Oscar was a cat that kept appearing in the background. The film went straight to Blockbusters and soon disappeared.

Cameron set up an internet porn website. He's a multi-millionaire now. Dame Helen went on to greater success. In his final joke to Klimer, Brandon Farlow made another film before he passed away, letting *The Island of Dr Farquar's Fiends* slowly pass into oblivion. Lara did OK. After missing out on a few big films to Hollywood actresses, she did a lot of TV work, and ended up being the voice of a children's cartoon character. She spends most of her time attending schools to get the kids to read more. Geno Wright won an Oscar ten years after this film was made.

John Kurtis was finally found. He ended up making documentaries, most of
them about conspiracy theories, which became very popular from 2001. He finally was nominated for an Oscar, for a

documentary about some parrakeets that had escaped from the film set of The African Queen when it was being made in Borehamwood in the 1950's and were now taking over the suburbs.

And here I am today, older, wider, and only a slightly bit wiser. I am back on a beach and still in the film business (to a certain extent). I watch my kids come towards me. The eldest has the nickname of Reggie. They didn't like it, until they became a dreaded teenager, and then thought it was great. They have also taken up acting and have appeared in a few TV shows. I've told them not to do films until they've studied their craft properly and seen a bit of life.

I often look back at my time on the island. In the big scheme of things, it was just a small moment in what has been a long life. But like a scene from a film or a show, or a piece of music, and maybe even love, we remember them not because they are great, but because of how they made us feel at the time. And even if all I have now are memories, I don't mind. The future is all yours, but the past is mine.

Credits

8 1/2

12 Angry Men.

Amadeus.

An American Werewolf in London.

Andrei Rublev.

And then there were none. Agatha Christie.

Apocalypse Now.

Bill Hicks. Revelations.

Blackadder. TV series.

Breaking Bad. TV series.

Bridget Jones Diary. Helen Fielding.

Cat People.

Changes. David Bowie.

Chinatown.

Cinema Paradiso.

Confessions of a Pop Star.

Crime and Punishment. Fyodor Dostoevsky.

Critical Drinker.

Dr. No.

Eastenders (pre 1996, before Rollo died). TV series.

Fargo.

Father Ted. TV series.

Forest Gump.

Grange Hill. TV series.

The Godfather.

Hunky Dory. David Bowie.

Indiana Jones Trilogy.

Into the Mystic. Van Morrison.

The Island of Dr Moreau. H.G. Wells.

The Island of Lost Souls.

Journey's End. R. C. Sherriff.

Like Stories of Old. YouTube channel.

Local Hero. Original Soundtrack.

Lock stock and Two Smoking Barrels.

Lord of the Flies. William Golding.

The Lord of the Rings.

The Lost Island. TV series.

Lost Soul: The Doomed Journey of Richard Stanley's Island of Dr. Moreau

Maid Marion and her Merry Men. TV series.

Now That's What I call Music. Various artists.

Oh Crikey, Its Lawnmower Death. Lawnmower deth.

Only Fools and Horses. TV series.

On the Buses (film).

Planet of the Apes.

Porridge. TV series.

Portnoy's Complaint. Philip Roth.

The Queen is dead. The Smiths.

Quentin Tarantino.

Razzle.

Red Dwarf. TV series.

Run through the Jungle. Creedence Clearwater revival.

Samba Pa Ti. Santana.

Seize the Day. Saul Bellow.

The Shawshank Redemption.

Sgt. Bilko. TV series.

Sgt. Peppers Lonely Hearts Club Band. The Beatles.

Spaced. TV series.

The Sopranos. TV series.

Step on. The Happy Mondays.

Suavecito. Malo.

Sullivans Travels.

The Stone Roses.

The Spy Who Loved Me.

This is Spinal Tap.

Tarzan, Lord of the Jungle. TV series.

Trainspotting. Irvine Welsh.

Top of the Pops. TV series.

Urban Hymns. The Verve.

V for Vendetta.

What's the Story Morning Glory. Oasis.

White Lines. David Gray.

Withnail and I.

X Men.

Yojimbo.

The Young Ones. TV series.

Zardoz.

Printed in Great Britain
by Amazon